Tragic Detour

By: Sara Abbott

Jessica:
Sometimes life sends us on a tragic detour, but as long as we keep pressing on toward God we can be assured He will set us on a path that He has blessed!
Keep Pressin' On
♡ Sara Abbott

II

1

Without a Word

The roar of the crowd was rhythmic that night. The stomping of feet, clapping of hands, and the chants of the fans created a noise inside that gym that drowned out the worries of the world. I was the new face in the crowd, I was still trying to figure out everyone's story in that small town. My eyes panned the many faces in the gym, when suddenly the doorway was filled with the silhouette of a tall, handsome, scruffy faced farm boy. He was looking intently through the crowd. He was focused. He knew exactly what, or who, he was looking for. With the noise of the crowd and the people passing him like a revolving door, it was as if none of those things even phased him. The intensity of his focus drew me in. I caught myself just watching him, waiting to see what it was that was powerful enough to make a roaring gym feel like it was as silent as a church house. He continued to pan the crowd and within just a few minutes he stopped looking. He had found what it was he was looking for. I followed his gaze and realized his eyes were locked in with a beautiful blonde. Her skin was kissed by the sun, and her long blonde hair just drew you in. As I was observing her beauty, their eyes stayed locked in that position for what felt like minutes, but I'm sure it was just a few seconds. Their hearts were talking so loud it wasn't necessary for any words to be spoken. Right before my eyes, without a word, a beautiful love story began to unfold between the tall, handsome, rugged faced farm boy and the sun kissed blonde. Before she looked away from the doorway, that beautiful blonde couldn't help but flash that snow white smile his way, he raised his eyebrow and a small smirk smeared across his face. The buzzer, ending the second quarter, brought me back to reality. I left the gym that night still in awe of a love that loud, a love story so strong that it didn't even need a single spoken word.

I continued to blindly find my way through the town over the next week. I loved the view of that small town from the bottom of the hill on Main Street. The name of that street was Blakely Street, but it was definitely the main street of that small town. It was practically the only real street in that town. The dim street lights lit up the school, the church, and the gas station like magic. It reminded me of one of those Christmas villages that your grandma set up when she put up her Christmas decorations every year. You know the one. You stood so big above those little villages, and as you would stare down at the rubber streets that were made to look like bricks and the cotton she had placed around the sidewalk to make it look like snow, it was almost as if you could see little people down there, and you could only imagine what the story of that little town could be. Blakely Street would have been the perfect Christmas village, and there was not a lack for a story. The story of this town was unfolding right before my eyes, day by day, person by person. There was no mystery left for those that had walked these streets for years, some their whole lives, but for me mystery was everywhere. Behind every smile, there was a story. Behind every kind, friendly, surface word, there was a real person who was just coming out of a storm, heading into a storm, or right in the middle of the storm. I waded my way blindly through, as questions constantly raced through my mind; where would I fit, who was it that would be my group of friends, or would this be a time of life where I would journey alone? Would I find my place here? All of these things played through my mind every time I drove through town, sat at a basketball game, or walked the halls to pick my kids up from school. The mystery of that farm boy and the sun kissed blonde would creep in, too. It was still just there, lingering, occupying space and fueling curiosity.

In those few days between that first game in the gym and the next one on the schedule, I received a phone call. "Hello?," I answered. On the other end, a happy voice with a sweet southern draw greeted me, "Hey, Haley. This is Rachel, I'm Peyton's mom." She paused for just a few seconds. In that short split second, I was trying to rack my brain, *Peyton... Peyton... Peyton, which kid was this?* Then it registered, my oldest daughter Katie had talked a lot about her friend Peyton. In the moment of silence, as this registered to me, she continued, "I'm wondering if you would be interested in helping me coach the girls' basketball team at school?" I delayed my response as I was trying to think of reasons to say no. I figured if I waited a few more seconds she would either hang up, or totally give me an out. Neither one of those things happened so I laughed and said, "Girl, I don't know much about basketball, but I'm happy to help you out!" She never hesitated and quickly replied, "Ok, great! I'll see you at practice on Monday."

Monday night I stepped into that old gym. The stale smell of gym shoes and junior high kids who lack the motivation to apply deodorant, lingered in the air. I walked in and immediately felt the need to hold my breath, or pinch my nose, in hopes of not smelling that rank stench. I was contemplating my decision and as I looked up, there she stood. The radiating blonde, flashing that snow white smile my way, stood at the other end of the court and threw me the ball. She broke the silence with that sweet southern voice and said, "Let's get started!" In that short hour we spent together at practice that night, I quickly figured out that this blonde haired, long legged beauty was fun and full of life. That stunning smile was something she wore often, and she wore it well. She was competitive at all cost. She didn't care if you were five or thirty-five, if you said we were keeping score, she was going to win. Rachel and I stood on the sidelines and told the girls to get on the line so they could run and get their conditioning in. I walked over to the heavy, squeaky door and opened it to let the cool, crisp air in. After I opened the door, I headed back to stand next to Rachel. She had a whistle in her mouth and every time the girls got back to the line and rested for just a few seconds she would blow the whistle again. I followed the girls, with my eyes only, of course. I wouldn't have been running those drills unless I was being a chased by a bear. As my eyes followed them to the other side of the court, something in the doorway caught my eye. The farm boy filled the doorway just as boldly as he had a few nights ago. I anticipated their loving gaze and even their warm embrace. It was as if romantic music was playing in my head as I waited, then the most unexpected piece of reality shattered that moment of anticipation for me. That sweet southern voice broke through the silence and said, "Girls, get the bags out of the jeep, Dad is here to pick you up." She hugged and kissed those two sweet girls, and they disappeared into the darkness with that tall, rugged faced farm boy, that I now knew to be Jack Wayne. Rachel and I stood there for a few seconds, in what felt like awkward silence, then walked out together. As we walked, I was trying to figure out what had just happened. The words just fell out of my mouth with a little heartache, but no resistance, "Wow, I had no idea you guys were divorced?" My mind was racing, my heart was breaking; and I felt like the air had just been knocked out of me. The week before I had witnessed these two find each other in an over-crowded, fan-raging gym and communicate with their eyes and hearts so loudly that I left feeling like I had just read an intense romance novel without one spoken word. Now this blonde beauty was standing in the dimly lit playground, just outside that old gym, telling me that her and the tall, handsome, scruffy faced farm boy were divorced. Tonight was the first time this woman and I had exchanged words, so I tried to hold back the eruption of emotion and disappointment I felt. There was no refraining the thoughts racing in my mind and the instant pain that my heart was experiencing. Rachel and I entered the gym that night as two moms coaching our daughters' ball team. We left that night bonded by an unspoken burden that was heavy with misery, pain, and regret, and now I was bearing it with her.

The next week as I pulled up to that old, red brick gym, the noise of the crowd was just as loud as it had been the week before. I walked up the steep wooden stairs, greeted by that stunning smile and contagious laugh. I sat down next to Rachel that night anticipating our girls' performance at half time. We waited for the first two quarters of the game to pass. We talked and laughed, and in just an instant, her smile faded just a bit. She looked distracted all of the sudden. I followed her eyes as they quickly moved to the doorway. I glanced at the doorway, and there he stood. His tall, lean stature, scruffy face, and dirty boots filled that doorway just as it had the week before. He looked up into the crowd, intently looking for the sparkle in her eyes and the beauty of her smile. It didn't take long, he had found her, their eyes locked once again. The intensity of their gaze was so strong, it felt as if the gym were empty and just the three of us stood there trapped in that moment. Time had frozen, their hearts raged with pain and regret as they were writing another chapter of their broken, sad, love story, without one single word. After what felt like hours, but I'm sure was just a few seconds, Rachel looked away. It was as if the death grip of reality snuffed her out. She was normally radiating like the sun, but in that moment the darkness of their reality had eclipsed the light inside of her. The joy and love that normally oozed out of her had been overshadowed by the darkness of their reality. Silently they suffered, and each one thought to be imprisoned in their pain and regret alone, but it appeared that they were there together, longing for each other, longing for healing, and longing to transform the darkness of their reality. That night as that cloud of darkness hung over them, there was still that light in her eyes when she saw him, and he was still looking for her in a crowded room. There were just so many pieces of this puzzle that didn't quite make sense yet, and maybe they never would, but as I started settling in that small town, I realized I was not alone among the walking wounded.

The old, stuffy gym became our meeting place. A few nights a week we would meet there to practice. Tthe other few nights a week we would meet there to watch our baby girls perform their ball handling tricks and jump rope routine.   It had been several weeks now since that first Monday night practice in the gym. Rachel and I had engaged in many conversations, but never a word about the burden we now carried together. The burden was there, and we were both very aware of it. It was almost as we talked around it, to avoid the unknown of what the conversation would sound like. Jack wasn't a man of many words. He and I had barely spoken, more the less about the fact that just from outward observation I could tell he was still in love with this small town girl with the sun kissed skin and the contagious laugh. Jack was guarded and somewhat mysterious. I couldn't get a good read on him at all, other than the one I got as he stood in that doorway gazing at that blonde beauty. He was dry and almost had an arrogance about him it seemed.   That was definitely the read my husband, Jason, got on him. Jason was also a quiet guy, a listener, and an observer. He had several observations about Jack, and surprisingly had a very vocal opinion, which wasn't like Jason normally. He told me one night, "That Jack Wayne is just an arrogant jerk." Maybe he was, maybe that is why they weren't together anymore, I had no idea actually. To be honest all I could think about when I saw them was how they were able to love each other so much and be lying their heads down on separate pillows every night under separate roofs.

2

Echoes of Love

The uncertainty of who Jack Wayne really was beneath his arrogant exterior and his inability to communicate much with words was all erased one cold night in February. A good month or so had passed since Rachel and I met that night in the old gym and I watched the farm boy walk out into the darkness with those two sweet girls. Rachel and I had spent about four nights a week together at practices and Saturdays at games. She was still hiding her heart. I wasn't sure how wounded she was, how they got to this place, and how, or if, they wanted to get back to sleeping in the same bed, under the same roof, and sharing the same name. I did know that trust between us was building.

It was Jack's week to have the girls. He came walking in through the famous doorway where he often stood and brought the girls in to practice. I had never known him to stay at practice, or even come in, unless he was picking them up. So it surprised me to see him there. He dropped the girls' bags that he had carried in and said, "Hey y'all need some help!" At first, I thought he was asking us if we needed his help. I quickly realized that he was making a statement, not asking a question. Before we could even answer him, he continued confidently, "Because, obviously, y'all can't coach!" He smirked his crooked, little, ornery grin and sat down on the bench. We had not experienced many victories with those sweet little 4th and 5th grade boys and girls. I was certain that our lack of success was due to my inability to coach. Rachel was a great ball player and an amazing athlete. I, on the other hand, could show them how to do a herkie to celebrate, if we could even make a shot to constitute such a celebration. Jason's words at this point began haunting me. I'm thought, "*Man this guy is a total jerk!*" I really wanted to give him the benefit of the doubt, but that benefit was expiring as he sat over there, still smirking, so proud of himself for the sweet comment he had just made to us. Rachel never missed a beat, didn't hesitate a bit, and quickly accepted his offer. I'm not sure he was actually making an offer, I think he was just taking the chance to make fun of our amazing losing streak, but Rachel didn't care. In that sweet southern voice, she said, "C'mon, let's go!" as she bounced him the ball. At first I was somewhat relieved. I was thinking, *Thank you Jesus, this may get me out of coaching, maybe he actually knows what he is doing.*" On the other hand, I was thinking, "*GIRL, tell this jerk NO!!*" As I was playing out all this dialogue in my head, my thoughts were interrupted with real conversation, "C'mon Haley. We are gonna scrimmage the kids, us against them," Rachel said. I wanted to ask her, "*Is this a joke?*" Not only do we now have to spend the next hour with this guy, she wants us to be his teammates. I smiled through my thoughts and politely said, "Ok, let's do it," with a lot of sarcasm and a bit of forced excitement.

Their oldest daughter, Baylee, was a spitting image of her Mama. She was only twelve, but her long, blonde, beautiful hair and long, skinny legs made her appear to be much older. Right before we got started, Baylee began to beg Rachel to play with us, "Mom, let me play on y'all's team!!" Rachel just looked at her with a slightly raised eyebrow and a sweet little smirk on her face. You could see that Rachel was contemplating the yes, as Baylee continues to plea her case. Jack immediately interrupted the contemplation process and as dry as the Arizona desert says, "No you're not playing with us, you're not an adult!" The description that Jason had so confidently laid out for me of this Jack Wayne character was ringing in my head like an old school bell; selfish, arrogant, jerk! Man, I hated to admit when my husband was right. The farm boy's big, goofy smile intercepted my thoughts. He flashed his teeth at Baylee, bounced her the ball and said, "Show 'em what you got!" She smiled a playful grin back at him and the games began.

In that hour, I watched as they played as a team, a good team. A team that had played many hours together before. A team that anticipated the play of the other before it even happened. I realized two things that night when I left the gym: First, Jack Wayne was not an arrogant jerk. He was a very broken man, whose heart was bleeding outside his chest and he was the walking wounded. He loved Rachel and his two girls with every ounce of his being. He liked to hide his heartache behind his hard exterior so that people wouldn't see the agony that he walked in. He feared that letting that wall down would reveal to the outside world that the flesh of his wound was still fresh and that his heart may just be irreparable. He was afraid of vulnerability and he was afraid of the pain of healing. Healing, at the end of its process, is a place we all want to be, but the steps to healing are normally painful. When you have a cut, an open wound, the first step is to clean it. The pain and suffering that occurs when that first drop of alcohol or peroxide is poured onto a wound is sometimes unbearable. Then there is the scab stage, when a wound scabs over, and God is doing a healing on the inside, and so He has placed a protective layer over the outside as He works. So many times we get impatient and we want to peel that scab off before the healing has happened, and then we delay the process of healing. Jack Wayne was so fearful of the initial sting that he hadn't even begun to heal. He would rather roam around wounded and trapped in his emotions of failure and loss than feel the pain of healing. The second thing that I learned that night was that those two girls, Baylee, the spitting image of her Mama, and Peyton, the spitting image of her Daddy, were so happy for that hour in time that they were a family again. In the sixty minutes that ticked away as we played that game, their pain was numbed from their broken reality. With each basket made and each pass thrown, they were not aware of the fact that they would go home to different houses. Their mom would drive away alone in her jeep tonight, and they would head back to dad's house. For those sixty minutes, reality didn't exist to those two girls. All that mattered is they played the game that night with their mom and their dad. As I came to those two realizations, the burden that I had already been bearing for Rachel got even heavier, and I might have picked up a load for Jack, too.

The next week we met in our usual spot, sitting in those hard wooden bleachers, but there was something different about tonight. I walked through the doorway of the gym, the one that normally occupied that scruffy faced farm boy, who was now more than just a man in the doorway to me. I immediately spotted Rachel and her radiating smile and golden blonde hair. As Jason and I began making our way toward her, she waved big, and was making room for us to sit by her. There were people all around. The gym seemed more crowded than usual. I braved my way through the crowd and up the steep bleachers. She reached her hand down to help pull me make the big step up. Before I could even take a seat, she said, "Hey girl, I want you to meet someone, this is my husband, Mike." I can't imagine what my face was saying, because my heart was breaking and my mind was screaming out in disbelief. I was afraid to speak, fearful that what was raging in my mind would possibly slip right out of my mouth. I reached out my hand to shake his, and tried to compose a fake smile. Thankfully, Jason reached his hand out next, and said, "Hey man, nice to meet you!" I sat down trying to gather my thoughts which were so scattered. It would probably take days to accomplish that. What was happening? I just knew that the small town girl with the sun kissed skin and snow white smile loved that rugged faced farm boy. They were going to get back together and their family was going to be whole again, I just knew it. Well, that is what I knew before the reality of this moment crashed through shattering that expectation. She was remarried? She was Jack's girl, she belonged to him. I had seen the way their hearts had spoken to each other without one word. I had seen it many times now. I wasn't sure how her heart had not informed her head that she was not free to give herself to anyone else. She had given her heart to Jack a long time ago and she had failed to get it back!

There was much conversation that game, almost like overcompensated conversation for the unspoken awkwardness that was lingering with us in the gym that night. I engaged in conversation, but I can't remember one word spoken. My body was sitting on the bleachers that night, but my heart and my mind were not in attendance. My heart and mind, they had checked out. They were on a field trip back to the practice that we had attended just a week ago. That practice where we were all on the same team, against my will, but I had to admit, it was great. The practice where Jack and Rachel and their girls were a family for sixty minutes. The practice where I thought, healing is definitely on its way to this family. That's the field trip my heart and mind were on as my body sat in the pain stricken presence of reality. The final buzzer rang. The game was finally over. We stood gathering our things, and were interrupted by erupting laughter and loud, squeaky voices, "Mom, Mom, can Katie and Lexi spend the night, please?" Baylee and Peyton stood at the bleachers batting their beautiful little eyes at their Mama. Rachel was quick to respond, "Well, I sure don't care, you'll have to ask their mom." Immediately, Baylee, Peyton, Katie, and Lexi were all batting their eyes, begging to spend the night. I looked at Jason, he nodded as if he didn't care. I looked at Rachel, who was looking at me with sheer anticipation, and I said, "Are you sure you want all these kids at your house?" She laughed that contagious laugh and said, "Girl, I don't care, I'm going to bed when I get home, I don't care what they do!" So I looked at those four sets of puppy dog eyes, and reluctantly said, "Well, I don't care then!" I gave the girls the usual instructions, be good, listen, and act like a civilized child. I hugged Rachel and told her I would see her in the morning at the girls' game.

Jason and I left the gym, headed to the car, and decided we would run to town for a late night snack since we didn't have any kids to put to bed. Just about thirty minutes had passed since we had left the gym and my phone started ringing, it was Rachel. "Hey girl, does Jason know anything about plumbing? We have a water leak," she asked with a giggle in her voice. She never had a doom, gloom moment. I asked Jason, he said, "Yeah, tell them we are on our way." We turned the truck around and headed south. Jason and I began to talk about the situation with Jack and Rachel, and our new found player to the game, Mike. Jason did not attend practice with me the night that Jack was there, the night that I realized that Jack was more than the arrogant persona that he was hiding behind. So Jason's opinion remained about Jack, which could nicely be summed up in two words, "Arrogant Jerk." There was no swaying Jason in his opinion, and he firmly stood on what he felt was fact. The only thing we agreed on during that conversation was that we were both still puzzled by how they could scream with their body language that they still loved each other, but they were divorced.

It was late and very dark as we made it to Rachel and Mike's house. Mike met Jason outside where the plumbing problem was, Rachel and I headed in the house where another problem awaited us. The girls were in the back playing, and Rachel and I began to talk. The fire was roaring, it was nice and cozy in there, and we just sat on the couch making small talk. My mind, of course, was doing what it normally did when I was around her, it was racing with curiosity and disbelief all at the same time. It had finally raced to the place that I could no longer contain my thoughts, and without me even realizing it, it just slipped right out of my mouth, "Girl, I don't know how you and Jack were married so long, and now are so nice to each other, and it doesn't make you think, man we should get back together?" I said this with a very light heart and a joking tone. I was not expecting a woman I had known for a couple of weeks to bear her soul to me, technically I was a stranger. I was just making conversation. I was expecting a slight explanation of why they weren't together, and honestly, I was anticipating her to say, "He's a big arrogant jerk, we play nice for the kids!" I turned to look at Rachel, as I was not hearing any response. She was sitting there, the fire was reflecting the tears streaming down her face. My eyes finally met hers and my heart stopped for a brief second. She was sobbing, wiping her eyes frantically. She finally began to speak, "It was a mistake, I made a mistake!" She continued to plead her case to me. What she didn't realize is she didn't need to say anything to me, I had already been reading their story every week they watched each other in the gym! She continued on, "If we communicated then, like we do now, we would still be married. We both just made some mistakes, but I want him back, I want my family back, I want my life back." In that moment I was stunned. I am not sure why. I knew all the things that she was saying, but finally hearing them in words was even more powerful than watching it play out without them. The unspoken burden that I had been carrying with Rachel just got heavier, and before I could even say a word, the door knob began to turn. She quickly wiped her eyes and we both immediately started talking about the girls, as if they had been the topic of conversation the whole time. Mike and Jason came in. She greeted him, as if nothing had ever been said and happily asked, "Y'all get it fixed?" Well, we think so," Jason answered. We got up, hugged briefly and had a conversation of our own without words. I headed to the door, and Jason and I walked quietly out to the truck. Jason and I got in, buckled up, and I just sat in silence for a few minutes, staring out the windshield, without even blinking. Silence was not something I practiced frequently, if ever, so Jason immediately asked, "What's wrong?" I answered slowly with sadness and heartache in my voice, never looking his way, continuing to just stare out the window, "She loves Jack, but she's married to Mike."

No matter how loud the gym was or how chaotic life seemed, after that day, I could hear echoes of the life Jack and Rachel once shared. The echoes of their past, the passion of the love they shared, it rang so loud through the brokenness they wore on their faces and their struggle to love again. It seemed that every time I stepped foot inside the gym, I begin to walk in the door with an expectation. I expected another heartbreaking piece of their tragic love story to come crumbling down on me. Today was no different, my expectation was met. I walked into the gym. I found comfort in the familiarity of my normal routine. I found my seat next to Rachel and anticipated the moment of heartbreak as tense as I am when I'm anticipating the drop at the top of a roller coaster. Just like the roller coaster, it doesn't matter how tense you get in the anticipation of the drop, it doesn't change the fact that it is still going to happen. I could anticipate the heartbreaking news of their love story as much as I wanted, it didn't change the fact that the painful pieces of their past were evident everywhere.

Jack made his way in the gym that night. He was cleaner in appearance than normal. He wore a black zip up jacket, that old ball cap bearing the label of his cattle company, and a clean shaven face. These things weren't the only thing different about Jack Wayne that night. He didn't stand in the doorway and gaze intently at Rachel, he just made a few quick glances and sat down. He wasn't his normal self, he was a little antsy, and not as bold and arrogant as he normally seemed. I don't know that I had ever seen him sit at a ball game. He was always standing in that doorway, or mysteriously walking around, but never sitting. He made his way just a few bleachers in front of us, and sat next to a tall, skinny, dark haired woman. I was trying not to stare at them the entire game, but I was trying to figure out who this woman was! Maybe this was a new girlfriend, or maybe it was his sister. His body language wasn't really screaming, "We're together." It really wasn't screaming anything.

Jack didn't wear a wedding ring, and I had never seen him with a woman before. All the practices and games I had seen him at, it was just him. I wanted so badly to lean over and ask Rachel who the girl was, but Mike was sitting right next to her and I didn't feel comfortable engaging in a conversation about Jack with him sitting right there, especially after Rachel's confession to me a few nights before. My mind was torturing me, and my eyes were locked on Jack and whoever she was, like super glue. I wanted to look away but I just couldn't without knowing who this woman was. Mike's voice ripped my eyes away as he broke the silence, "Hey, I'm going to go down and grab something to drink, do y'all want anything?" I wanted to yell, "YES, I want to know who the woman is sitting next to Jack Wayne." I was screaming that so loud in my head, I forgot to respond with my words. I'm assuming after a few minutes of awkward silence, Rachel bumps me with her elbow, "Hey girl, want a drink?" "Oh, no thanks," I reply as I told my mind to be quiet so my mouth could respond. I just couldn't wait for Mike to make his way to the concession stand so I could ask Rachel who the girl was sitting with Jack. Their body language remained the same, non-existent. I had even almost ruled out sister. There was no teasing, or joking, really no interaction that I had seen. I had looked away for a slight moment to respond to Mike, so maybe I missed something. Mike made it to the bottom of the bleachers, not even through Jack's vacant doorway, and I leaned down and whispered to Rachel, "Who's the girl?" She squints her eyebrows and looks at me clueless. She pans the crowd briefly looking for who I might be talking about. I try to discreetly nod my head toward Jack. She smiles that big radiant smile, chuckles just a little as she looks his way, and responds, "That's his wife!" I tried to keep my voice to a whisper but man it was hard, "WHAT?!" I loud whispered back in more disbelief, as my eyes almost popped out of my head. "But he doesn't wear a wedding ring. I have never seen him with a woman, and I have seen him a lot over the past few months." I paused for a brief moment, I had more to plead my case of why this couldn't be his wife, but still wearing that big, white, beautiful smile, Rachel cut me off with her next response, "Well she has been home with the baby, he's only a couple of weeks old." I'm not sure what it feels like to be shot, but in that moment, I could maybe imagine. All the air left my lungs, my heart was residing in the bottom of my stomach. The world my mind escaped to was as silent as a church during a funeral. There is no way I could have prepared properly for a drop like this. Although it didn't matter whether I anticipated it or not. Reality is no respecter of person or circumstance, and reality had just come raging through my heart with a dagger.

Jack Wayne, the farm boy, who still loved Rachel, the beautiful, small town girl, who radiated with kindness and grace, was married and had a new baby? How was it that Rachel occupied Jack's heart, but this woman occupied his bed? So many questions and I'm not sure there were answers. How did they get here, tangled up in a mess of decisions that kept them locked away from each other in a prison of pretending, drowning in the pain of regret? I can't remember the outcome of the game that day, but the outcome for the farm boy was a loss in the game of love. Just as the voices and the sounds of the game echoed in the gym that night, so the love of their past echoed through every waking moment of their lives. The raging echoes made it impossible for them to truly love with their whole heart. They were trying, pretending, and existing in their current circumstances. The echoes haunted their lives with every attempt to step forward. They constantly battled the overwhelming desire to look back. To give in to the desire meant to see the pain of their past, the residue of the life they had built, and the ashes of the dreams they once shared. Every time they tried to begin building new dreams, with each brick, there was a piece of their past in every drop of mortar. She was a part of that farm boy and he was a part of her. Even though they had gone their separate ways, there were parts of her that would forever be woven in him, and parts of him that would always be a part of her. The facts were that over fourteen years ago, on a scorching hot day in August, that farm boy made that blonde beauty his wife and they became one flesh. Through divorce, they tried to tear themselves away from each other, yet remnants of their flesh remained. There was one thing left in life I believed to be the absolute truth, and that was the Bible. God's Word, The Good Book, whatever label you choose to give it doesn't change the power that lies within it. "So they are no longer two, but one flesh. What God has joined together, let no one separate." (Matthew 19:6) They might have gotten separated physically, and even signed a piece of paper stating they were divorced, but what God had joined together, well there was no complete separation of that. When they chose to rip their flesh apart, the consequences of that divorce were that pieces of their hearts, minds, and souls would forever remain together. As the days continued to pass us by, the echoes of their love were ringing louder and louder through all of our lives.

3

The Soundtrack of Tragedy

The next couple of weeks would find us all together again in the old gym. With every encounter the echoes of that love story were so loud I didn't know how much longer Rachel could bear the weight of her regret, the noise of her past, and the pain of pretending. I was trying to embrace the fact that Rachel was married to Mike, not Jack. I really liked Mike, he was a very nice guy. Mike seemed almost the complete opposite of Jack in many areas. Jack was a tall, rugged faced, simple man. He was not a man of many words. Mike was much shorter in stature than Jack, he was smaller framed, his face was completely clean shaven, and he wore a big white smile to match Rachel's. He was a talkative guy, with much more personality than Jack, although that didn't seem like it would take much. I was certain a paper bag would give the farm boy a run for his money. I wanted to believe that Rachel really loved Mike, but when Jack Wayne made his way to the doorway in the gym, it was so obvious that Rachel's heart would always belong to him. I didn't even know how to wrap my mind around the latest reveal about Jack, his wife Alivia, and their little baby boy Avery. I was so curious to see inside that man's soul. Was he pretending? Was he conflicted? Did he love Alivia? Or was Alivia a band aid who was there for his wounded soul when Rachel ripped his heart out and left his world wrecked and in complete chaos? I knew where Rachel stood, I knew that she was being held prisoner in the darkness of her regret and misery. How could Mike and Alivia not see what we all were seeing? Or could they? Surely I wasn't the only one who could read the dialogue in a crowded gym between their hearts? There had to be others, they just weren't brave enough, or stupid enough to say anything out loud. I hadn't had enough time in this quaint little town to make close enough friends with anyone yet to ask them what in the world was going on. I knew in a town of this size someone had to know what was going on, or at least they thought they knew. Since I had no inside sources to contact, I just sat silently and suffered for these two, actually for all four of them. It was just a sad situation. I was sad for Jack and Rachel as it appeared they were living in regret. I was sad for Alivia and Mike, I had no idea what state they were living in, but I had a feeling that the truth was going to come ripping through their world through the echoes of the love that was still beating in the hearts of Jack and Rachel.

Jason and I made our way into the gym, another night meeting in our place. The air was crisp and cool that night, we could see our breath outside in the darkness. We headed to the concession stand to find some coffee to help us warm up. Out of the corner of my eye, I saw that long, blonde ponytail hanging out of her white golf ball cap she always wore. I leaned down to lightly pinch her side. "Hey, girl!" I said as I greeted her. She jumped, and then quickly turned around with that stunning smile, and said, "Hey girl!" with that deep southern drawl in her voice. We hugged briefly got our coffee, and made our way up the bleachers where Mike was waiting. We had just settled in our seats, when above the noises of the gym, I heard a loud, happy voice, quickly approaching us. I looked up to see the face matching the voice. As the woman approached us she leaned down to hug Rachel. She then made her way to Mike and hugged him as well. The beautiful woman with dark, curly hair was followed by a tall, handsome man in a ball cap that hid his silver white hair. She stepped right in front of me and said, "Hi, I'm Kathy and this is Buck!" I shook their hands and told them it was nice to meet them. She said likewise, and then quickly took a seat right behind us. We stood to our feet to sing the National

Anthem. I placed my hand over my heart then I tried to subtly lean over to Rachel and whisper in her ear, "Is that your Mom?" There was no whisper or subtleness in her response. Her head flew back, her mouth was wide open and that contagious laugh came belting out. She turned to look me directly in the eye, which was good, because I was afraid to look anywhere else in fear the whole gym was staring at us, and she said, "No, girl, that is Jack's Mom."

I wasn't up for much conversation once we sat down. I was trying to figure out how this beautiful, dark haired woman, comes up the bleachers with complete genuine love and kindness, hugs her EX daughter-in-law and her new husband, and then takes her seat right behind us. I couldn't help but think that at any moment Jack would make his way through that doorway, boldly climb those old wooden bleachers, kiss Rachel's beautiful face, shake Mike's hand, and take his seat next to his Mom. I mean seriously, I felt like I was watching a movie. Was this really happening? What was happening? Once again another piece of their tragic love story revealed itself and here I was trying to figure out how these pieces ever all fit together the first time and would they fit together again? These thoughts had led me away from the game once again, and although physically I sat on those wooden bleachers with an aching booty, emotionally and mentally I was absent. All I could hear that night was the heartache of a broken hearted farm boy longing to love that small town girl once again. A tap on my shoulder broke me free from the piercing pain of the soundtrack their tragic love story was playing once again in my head. I turned around and Kathy was smiling at me. She asked inquisitively, "So are you guys liking it here in Rush Springs?" "Oh yes ma'am, we are loving it here," I replied. I was friendly, yet distant. I wasn't sure if we liked Kathy. My loyalty lied with Rachel, and I didn't know what the situation was between her and Kathy, Jack's mom. I didn't know if Rachel really liked Kathy, or if she was just kind to her because of her girls. I was proceeding in my conversation with Kathy, with extreme caution. Well, that was my strategy, but it was quickly derailed. Kathy was anything but distant. She talked with me that night like I had known her my entire life. Kathy was the kind of woman that loved with her whole heart. She didn't love with a heart of stone, like many of us do. As life hands us pain and heartache, we begin to put stones all around our heart, protecting it from the possibility of future pain, yet prohibiting it from truly loving. Kathy had a heart of flesh and if life had handed her pain, she hadn't allowed the pain to become bricks around her heart. I longed to love that way. But every time life had sent pain and heartache my way, I quickly placed those hard learned lessons around my heart in fear. I didn't want to feel pain, rejection, or abandonment, ever again in life, so I felt leaving my heart behind the walls was the safest bet for me. It was the safest choice, but it wasn't the choice that would bring healing, and it was a very lonely choice.

Over the next few weeks Saturday became my favorite day. A few nights a week landed us in the gym to watch the girls perform their ball handling skills and their jump rope routines, but Saturdays landed us in the gym to coach. The coaching wasn't the fun part for me, since I didn't know much about basketball, but spending time with the girls, Rachel, and Kathy, were the things I looked forward to the most on Saturdays. Thankfully, what I learned about Kathy, from the first night I met her in the gym, was that Jack and Rachel still shared a few things; custody of the girls was one of them and a relationship with Kathy was another. I loved to be around Kathy. She just made life better. It was unquestionable why Rachel chose to keep Kathy in the divorce. Once you were loved by Kathy, you were never the same. To walk away from a love powerful enough to change your life would be a crippling mistake, but to do it twice in a lifetime would be a death sentence. Rachel had left a love that held that kind of power when she left Jack, and she now walked through life handicapped from the scars that choice had left her with. She valued her life enough to fight to keep the love she had from Kathy, the love that had the power to mend a broken heart, the strength to carry the walking wounded, and the immensity to change your life. As each day passed I had the privilege of feeling that kind of love from Kathy, and before I knew it my life was changed as well. One day at a time, her love began to remove another stone that had surrounded my heart for so long.

It was a beautiful spring morning as we drove to the gym that particular Saturday. I was met at the door by Kathy. Everyone that knew Kathy well called her KK. She always greeted you with a warm hug that could ignite a fire even in the coldest heart. Today was no different, she greeted me with that warm hug, and very excitedly questioned, "Hey, I'm wanting to have all the kids over for a sleep over next Friday night, would that be okay?" I knew the girls would be so excited to spend the night with Baylee and Peyton at KK's house, so without hesitation I said, "Sure, KK, they would love that!" KK immediately began to tell me her plan to fill the kids up on junk food, have a bonfire, and play games. She then gave me all the instructions and finished up her declaration of information by saying, "Just bring the girls' bags to my classroom Friday when you drop them off at school, I'll just take them from there!"

A lot took place that week from the invitation on Saturday morning to the night of the sleep over. Rachel and I had not spoken much more about her confession to me about her love for Jack. I don't know if we thought if we ignored it that it would just go away, but if that is what we thought, well we were wrong. Although we had decided to ignore that topic of conversation, the words that their hearts had exchanged without their mouths saying a word could not be ignored. Rachel had spoken her feelings out loud to me that night, but her mind was telling her that he was happier without her. My inability to read him made me unsure if her mind was telling her lies, and Jack wanted her back as much as she wanted him, or if he was ok staying locked in the pain and regret, but Jack's next move was about to take my uncertainty to complete clarity. Although Rachel carried the pain of her past and lived imprisoned with the reality that she couldn't express her love to him, without even realizing it, she was always looking for a glimpse of hope. Hope that there was a future for them, hope that she wouldn't serve a life sentence separated from the only person she had ever given her heart to, a hope that somehow, someway, they would find their way back to each other. With one little sound of the phone, informing her of an incoming text message, that spark of hope ignited. She looked down at the screen and read his name. As she read his name, her heart skipped just a bit. She opened the text message and it simply said, "100.5". She quickly turned her radio to the station that he had sent. Although the text message had simply stated the radio station, the words coming through that radio from the heart of that farm boy to that small town girl were anything but simple. *Don't you cry tonight; I still love you baby. Give me a whisper, and give me a sign, give me a kiss and tell me goodbye. Don't you take it so hard now, and please don't take it so bad, I'll still be thinking of you and the times we had baby.* The song played on and the tears continued to pour out of her beautiful blue eyes. Every time she allowed herself to think about the love she lost it was as if she stood in a cemetery staring at the headstone of their past and now with the simple chorus of a song, it seemed there was hope for resurrecting their love.

Once again, the sweet sensitivity of this man who hid behind a hard, arrogant persona expressed to the love of his life that although they may never be together again, he still loved her, and once again, he did it without a spoken word. Several months before this text ignited hope for Rachel, she had heard a song and wanted to send it to Jack but she didn't in fear that he didn't feel the same way about her. Once the hope was ignited, the impulse of emotion took over her and she immediately sent the song that had haunted her head as she lay down in the stillness of the nights, and in the silence of every moment. The song that had made her heart ache for him just few months before. She managed to see through the tears and type one of the songs that had now made the list on the soundtrack of their painful love story, *I miss the simple conversations, I miss the silence in between, I miss the clatter in the kitchen, it always seemed to help me sleep, but most of all I miss you. I know I drew a line in the sand that I can't cross back over, I know baby you'll be fine, but if you don't mind I'll never recover.*

Jack wasn't a man of many words, nor a man that had shed many tears, but as he read the words to the song, his heart was happy, his eyes welled up with tears and for just a few seconds they both escaped the pain of their reality with the pondering of what might have been. This was a day of great clarity for both of them.

This day was a revelation that although physically they were not together, their hearts would always beat as one.

With the joy of their revelation came the painful stab of reality. Now they no longer walked in the darkness and the mystery of the love they lost. They walked in the light of the confession, but also in the pain of what used to be, the haunting echoes of what might have been, and the impossible task of figuring out how to put the pieces of their shattered lives back together again. In a sense, the confession was either the beginning of a long road back home, or it was just another painful piece of the sobering truth of their circumstance. Only time would tell which direction the detour would take them from here. The confidence I once had for this journey to lead them back home to each other diminished, piece by piece, as their current situations were revealed to me. Rachel was married to Mike, and seemed to have accepted that although her heart belonged to Jack, she didn't feel that she deserved forgiveness, restoration, or true redemption. It was almost like she felt like staying locked in her prison of pretending was the life sentence she would serve for walking out on Jack. Jack now had a son, a child tangled in this web of love, pain, and regret. The truth of their circumstance was devastating, but the power of their love was optimistic in the face of the devastation.

The truth is powerful and freeing, you can stretch it, omit it, and spin it, but it remains. The truth of their journey, no matter which road they chose at this point, was that pain was waiting to meet them there.

4

There Came a Day

The confession, through the exchanging of songs, was like slowly peeling off a band-aid. Each day that the sun rose and it set, another small piece of the band-aid was removed. I was not aware of the song exchange, but I could see the burden that Rachel bore weighing heavier on her with each passing day. I wanted to just hug her and tell her to talk to me, but I could tell she was still trying to figure out if she could trust me, and that was okay. We continued to meet up at the gym, and then we decided the days we weren't meeting at the gym we would meet at the track. We said we were there to walk and to exercise, but really we were there to talk. The very first day we met up at the track was cold. We could see our breath and the cold inflicted pain in our fingertips and toes. I was obviously in desperate need of the exercise to be willing to walk in such conditions, and Rachel was in need of the friendship, because that sun kissed girl hated the winter. We hadn't made it one full lap around the track and Jack's name was the topic of conversation. It took only a few seconds from the mention of his name for the tears to begin to fall. It was simple to me, being on the outside, with no emotional attachment. I felt like she had already made her decision, well her heart had made the decision, her head was having a hard time complying with the instruction. Her heart was no doubt with Jack, and always had been. Her head was beating her up for hurting Mike, and her guilt clouded her ability to know which one was right. Anyone who has ever loved, knows that sometimes your head plays tricks on you to keep you from feeling the prolonged torture your heart is putting you through. We finished up our walking and talking that day with tears and a feeling of hopelessness.

The next day the sun had pierced through the clouds and warmed the day up a bit. It was a Friday, my day off. The girls were at school, I was getting some chores done, I had taken a break to make me some lunch. I stood at the kitchen sink looking out the window, bending the Lord's ear about how to help Rachel and Jack. What was the right thing to do in a situation as messy as this one? Was there a right or wrong, and if so what was the answer? I tried to pray and study and seek God for them, but I quickly realized that this was their journey, it was the road God was allowing them to walk. Although I could stand on the sidelines and cheer them on, spiritually, I couldn't lace up my sneakers and run this race for them, I couldn't understand it for them, and I couldn't make sense of it for them. All I could do was love them as they ran, walked, or crawled through this excruciating part of their journey. As the Lord and I were conversing about all of this, my thoughts were broken up by a reflection in the window, someone was pulling up the drive. I stood on my tippy toes and leaned forward as far as I could, trying to see who was pulling in the driveway. Just as my calves started to burn from standing on my tippy toes, I could see the headlights of Rachel's jeep pulling in. I went to the back door to greet her. I reached out to hug her, she squeezed me a little tighter than usual, and as she held on I could feel the weight of that moment and I hesitantly anticipated what was about to happen. As soon as I pulled away, my arms still holding hers, I said, "What's going on?" She smiled, choked back her tears, and tried to play it smooth, "Oh nothing girl, I just thought I would swing by for lunch." I could tell there was more, but I didn't want to pry the issue.

I fixed our plates and sat down at the table, at that point she had held it together as long as she could. Tears were welling up in her eyes and there were a few seconds of piercing silence. The tremble in her voice broke through the silence as she managed to get out three life changing words, "I told him." My heart was racing in anticipation as to what was about to happen, and despite the racing of my heart and mind there was a sense of relief. I don't really know why, because telling him would be just the beginning of many hard decisions and many more days of heartache. It didn't mean that the prison of pretending that they lived in was over, it just meant that at least her secret was no longer suffocating her, at least now she could breath and decide where to go from here. One day, three little words, had the power and potential to change the entire direction their life was going. She began telling me what she had shared with Jack that day. She continued to talk, but her words became just a rambling noise, my thoughts were drowning the sound of her voice out.

The power of the spoken word is unexplainable and somewhat incomprehensible. The existence of the entire earth was created with a spoken word. The tongue has the power to give life or death. Today her spoken words had resurrected a love that had appeared dead. Those same words that had given life to the love of their past, might have just been the words that would kill the love of their here and now. The noise of her voice had stopped and I looked at her with a lost look as she stared back at me with a look of desperation. She said, "What do I do now?" Without hesitation I replied, "You're going to have to tell Mike." She looked disappointed, as that was not the answer she was hoping to hear, then she said, "Tell him what?" Again without a moment of hesitation and complete confidence I said, "The truth!" I knew that the truth would set them free. I didn't think it was going to be a painless process, nor one that would be marked down in the books of life as simple, but I had never known freedom to be something that was free. The road to freedom was always paved with blood, sweat, tears, and a lot of sacrifice, but freedom was always worth the price. Today was no different. We hugged for a long time that day, tears poured from both of our eyes, and our hearts ached together, but as Rachel headed out of that driveway, she left alone. I was painfully reminded once again that I could not walk this road for her, I could walk along side of her and love her through it, but she must face this day and the hard days to come alone.

I went about my normal routine for the day, my heart was so heavy and my mind scattered about. Just as I was trying to get my mind off of it, my phone alerted me of a message. I walked over to read the words, "Alivia knows that Jack and I have been talking. She saw a text Jack had sent to a friend.... ugh, my heart is in my stomach!" As I finished reading the words on the screen my own heart was racing, my mind was confused, and my stomach was sick, and yet this wasn't even my storm. As fast as I could type I replied, "OMGosh, what did Alivia say?" Rachel replied, "i don't know much, he said he would try and talk to me later." We didn't talk much after that text, Rachel would soon be home from work, so we went back to texting about the girls and anything and everything other than her and Jack.

Later that night Rachel text me to ask if the girls could go spend the night at KK's. We made the arrangements and that Saturday mid-afternoon that blonde beauty came driving up that long gravel driveway once again. She got out of the jeep, ball cap, tennis shoes and actually a smile on her face. The smile wasn't a permanent fixture today, it slowly faded. The girls headed to the barn to swing as Rachel and I headed to the kitchen, where we had our best talks. As soon as we stepped foot into that kitchen I asked very curiously, "So did you tell Mike?" "No, not yet. I've been at my Mom's today, pretty much avoiding him!" she replied almost disappointed in herself. "But you're going to tell him, right?" I asked with a little bit of force. "Yes, I'm going to tell him, but what do you even say?" she questioned as I poured us a glass of tea. She was already tearing up at this point. "Well, I am going with what I've told you from the beginning. You are going to have to tell him the TRUTH!! I'm not saying it's going to be easy, but it's the only way," I said very matter of fact. She continued on, "I know, it's just so hard because I do love him, we have fun together, and really he hasn't done anything wrong, there is just one major thing missing...." She paused for a long time and the tears were now flowing steadily down her cheeks, and at the same exact time, we both said, "Your heart."

Her heart didn't belong to Mike because it was never hers to give away. When she was a 17-year-old high school girl, unscathed by the world, and dreaming of her Prince Charming, Jack Wayne made his entrance into her life, stole her heart, and to this very day he continued to hold it in his hands. She may have pretended to get over him, and pretended to give her heart to Mike, but the hard, honest truth was, pride kept her from doing what she should have done three years ago, and that was to go home to Jack. Her pride had persuaded her that it was better to be right than to be happy, and she would show Jack that she didn't need him. Anything that he had ever done wrong in their marriage would be held against him, and anything she had done wrong, well she didn't want to face, so rather than face up she decided to run. To run away from a love that had changed her life, a love that had brought her joy, and a love that had made her a mother. She had run just as long as she could, and when she fell down in the state of exhaustion, what she had realized is in the pain and persuasion of her pride she had left Jack, gotten remarried, and was now living a lie. As she sat along the sidelines of her own life, all she wanted was a do over. A chance to look in the face of pride and say, "Thanks, but no thanks! The price that comes with the pride of being right isn't a price I'm willing to pay today!"

Unfortunately, life doesn't work that way. When pride persuades us to make decisions that put us in the painful prison of the consequences attached to those decisions, there are no do overs. There is just a long road of pain and humility and regret.

Most people feel that it is something they deserve and they stay there in that prison; they allow the devil to continue to torture them with the decisions they made until he paralyzes them emotionally and spiritually, then bitterness and decay begin to eat away at them little by little. Rachel had decided that she couldn't do that anymore, so maybe she wouldn't get a do over and maybe she couldn't go back and undo all that had happened, but she was determined to not stay beat down on the ground, she would rise again and be strong, no matter the outcome.

I remember asking her that day, "So do you think you guys are going to get back together?" She said, "I don't know, but I do know that I will be a better person when all of this is over, and I don't think that I ever valued the meaning of marriage, and all of this is definitely showing me how!" So regardless of what was happening, growth was happening in her own life, and I am sure in the lives of the others involved. You can't put a price tag on a few things in life, and growth is one of them. We are either growing or dying, stagnation isn't an option. Oh, if those kitchen walls could talk, we might be in trouble. Rachel and I stood up and hugged, shed a few tears, and as she headed out my driveway that day she headed south to KK's. I'm certain as she headed to KK's she was looking to find courage, the words to speak, and she was looking for her key to freedom that would unlock the prison cell of pretending that she was so painfully trapped in.

Rachel pulled up into KK's drive confused, torn, and even a little scared of what tomorrow would look like for her. There was magic at KK's though, so she had gone to the right place. Something happened to all your fears, your confusion, and your heartache when you sat at her table. As you sat at that old, long, sturdy, wooden table, you were facing a large picture window. Outside that big picture window, you could see the most beautiful purple flowers growing in a patch that almost looked wild. Not sculpted or cut to look a certain way or be a certain height, they were just free to be beautiful in the state they were in. Those flowers were kind of like all of us that darkened KK's door, looking for love, advice, or just a little help. She just scooped us up and loved us just the way we were, all wild, and crazy, she didn't try to cut us down, or prune us back, she just let us be. There was an amazing power in a love that had that kind of expression. Right past those beautiful purple flowers there was a long row of trees that had probably been there hundreds of years. They were full and tall, and secluded you from the view of the street. It was as if while you sat there getting your soul bandaged those trees served as a look out to protect you from the reality of the world that waited for you on the other side. No matter the wound, whether it was a wound of the flesh or of the heart, KK was always prepared to dress your wounds and help you get back on your feet. Today was no different.

Rachel had cried so many tears over the past couple of

weeks, one would think she didn't have many more to shed, but as she took her seat at that sacred table, KK sensed the sadness and asked Rachel, "Are you okay?" Rachel just shook her head no and in the safety and security that KK's presence created, the levy broke and the pain Rachel had been carrying for the past three years began rushing out. There were a few seconds of awkward silence, and for KK that was a few seconds too long, she didn't do silence well. She sat down at the table and put her arm on Rachel's shoulder, "Is this about what Jack told me yesterday about you two?"

Jack had been out of town, and when he had gotten home yesterday, the first stop he made was at his Mama's house. It doesn't matter who you are or how many birthdays you have celebrated, when a crisis arises you frantically find your way back home. Jack Wayne, although he hid behind that dry, hard exterior, was no different than the rest of us. Crisis had knocked with the song exchange, and he quickly opened the door. Now he wasn't sure how to get out of the mess he was in, and get to where he wanted to be, so Mama's house was the next stop. When Jack pulled up into KK's drive she knew something was going on with him. Although most of the time Jack suffered from constipation of communication and was very hard to read, there was no fooling Mama.

KK and Buck, better known as Pops, walked from the gravel drive out to meet Jack. They all walked together up to the calf barn. The walk was silent, and the atmosphere was somewhat tense with the anticipation that Jack would share with his parents what had brought him up their driveway that day. KK, being one who hated silence, tried to create small talk, although she knew the talk that awaited her, when he was ready, would be anything but small. "How was your trip son?" KK questioned. Jack quickly rushed his answers about the trip, and then the tension in the atmosphere was released like the air in a balloon. "I need to tell y'all something," he made this declaration as he had pre-rehearsed it a thousand times. He paused and waited for their response to set the mode for the confession that was about to happen. "Ok, what's going on, son?" KK questioned as her heart raced in fear of what was about to come out of her son's mouth. "I have made a real mess of things, a huge mess actually." He paused for just a few seconds, normally KK would fill that silence but she was somewhat in shock and paralyzed by the fear of what was about to follow. "I'm still in love with my ex-wife, I love Rachel. I have God first in my life, then Rachel, my kids, and then Alivia. We both feel the same, we want to get back together." Another few seconds of silence passed.

There is just a shock factor that exists when someone speaks those words. The information wasn't shocking to KK, she was reading the same tragic love story I had been reading without one spoken word. The difference is she had been reading it a lot longer than I had. You see love is powerful and mysterious, yet true love doesn't really need words. If I, just a stranger, practically could see and hear this love story unfolding, then his mother surely could. Again, it wasn't that KK was in the dark about how they had felt about each other, the shock was that their pain and regret had finally gotten so heavy that they decided they were not going to stay trapped beneath the pain and weight of it anymore. Breaking free from it all wasn't going to be easy though. It would be a process, one that would be long and must be handled with care. So many lives were now tangled in this web of love, denial, pain and pride. KK still had said nothing in response to Jack's confession, Pops had no words either, but that was the norm for him. Jack continued, "Y'all can have your thoughts and your opinions, but we are going to do what we want to do."

KK had finally gathered her thoughts enough to put together just a few words, "Well, son, that's pretty messed up. I don't even know what to say, I honestly don't even know how to pray for you, I'm just going to pray God's will and His guidance." KK's words were honest, yet graceful, and kind. She had not one drop of judgement in her response, it's just who KK was. No matter how dark or broken the road you were on, it didn't matter to her, she was there to love you, to dress your wounds, and to rescue you. They finished up their chores in the barn that night, not many words spoken. Under a blanket full of stars, they made their way back to the house. KK's heart was so heavy as she carried the burden for her son.

KK was always one to say what was on her mind, so as they made it to the porch, she asked Jack with sincerity, yet complete curiosity, "How did this happen, son?" Without one second of hesitation and complete confidence in his response Jack said, "I have never stopped loving her. I wake up thinking about her, I go to sleep thinking about her, and I dream about her. I have tried to ignore all of these feelings for so long, I have tried to lock them away, and I have even tried to tell myself that they don't exist, but I am tired of lying to myself, and lying to everyone else, I just can't do it anymore, Mom." KK didn't have the words to respond to such a declaration of love. So they finished walking home in silence, just the sound of the crickets could be heard. They took their seats on that porch swing together, sat in the dark, shed a few tears, and prayed wondering what tomorrow would bring.

Well, tomorrow was here, and it had brought Rachel up the same driveway that Jack pulled up to just one night before. The answer to KK's question that she had asked Rachel, if the tears were about the news she had heard yesterday from her son, the answer was yes. KK had tried yesterday to stay strong for her boy, but her strength was fading and her tears were forming. She was trying to blink back the tears, but she was failing miserably. She felt like her prayers were being answered, she had prayed for this. She had prayed for reconciliation, pride removed, and their family restored, but she felt like the answer was coming three years too late and she was heartbroken. Normally when prayers are answered there is rejoicing, but the fact that Jack and Rachel had moved on with their lives made it hard to know how to feel. Rachel was married, Jack was married, and he had a very new son. There was a deep sadness for Alivia and baby Avery, but KK had a sense of happiness for Baylee and Peyton. I'm not certain that in a situation as complicated as this that true clarity exists. Rachel had headed south that day to KK's to find comfort and clarity. I'm certain that she left her driveway with one of those thing, but clarity wasn't what she had found.

KK loved Rachel, she was the mother of her grandchildren. KK had spent sixteen years of her life with this beautiful girl. Rachel had grown up with KK. KK feared what this new found confession would do to their friendship. Rachel hurt Jack when she left him, and the pain that he suffered was felt by his Mama. They had finally come to a place of healing. Well, I don't know that it was a place of true healing, but they had put enough band aids on the situation that they were all getting along and trying to build relationships again. KK was fearful that these spoken words would rip the band aid off and friendships would be lost and relationships ruined.

The "what if's" of all of this circled around them like the

buzzards encompass the dead. It was a constant thought in everyone's mind, at every moment. But when KK allowed her heart to be vulnerable and naked, the truth was she was happy entertaining the thought of her kids getting back together. Her happiness was shattered when she began to think about what the road to making this a reality looked like. The road to restoration would be paved with heartache, brokenness, and pain. Getting back together wasn't as easy as it sounded. It would be excruciating pain for Mike and for Alivia, and even though Jack and Rachel would be getting the loves of their lives back, they were not the same people they were before this little detour. Jack Wayne would never be whole again this side of Heaven. Although getting back together with Rachel would mean getting his family back, it also meant losing his son, and a part of him would forever be with Avery, therefore that piece of him would forever be missing. It was all very messy and complicated.

Jack Wayne would pay a hefty price to get his old life back, he would be losing his son. This fact had to be haunting him, along with the reality that the detour that he and Rachel had been on the last three years was going to permanently cripple so many others emotionally. He had decided he was willing to pay that price. I was not unaware of the hurt that Jack and Rachel's decision was going to cause. They wore the hurt, and pain and sadness all over their faces. Jack knew he was going to hurt the mother of his son.

Unfortunately that was part of the price he had to pay for what he wanted. God would be the only one qualified to repair the immeasurable damage that this decision would bring to their life. Seeking Him would be the only way to heal the pain of such a wound and it would be the only way for them to find their road of restoration.

In not so many words, KK explained to Rachel that there would be a price for them to pay if this confession led them to walk the hard road of reality back home. Jack could lose the farm, the house, everything he had worked his entire life to build. There was a lot at stake, but at the same time Jack felt there was so much more to gain.

5

After Further Review

That night I was restless, I can't imagine how they were. I was praying, crying, begging the Lord for some kind of sign, some kind of direction. That next morning, I talked to Rachel and asked her if it was okay for me to send Jack a text. I felt like he needed to know that someone was praying for him. Rachel encouraged me to do so and thought it would be a good idea. Early that morning after I dropped the girls off at school, I sent Jack a text just letting him know that Jason and I would be praying for them as they struggled to figure out what to do next. His response was a short, "Thank you," which is really all I expected. After a few more minutes, he said, "So I guess this is Haley!" I confirmed my identity, and then he began to talk a little. Jack was sad, conflicted, and completely entangled in confusion. I had no idea how to help him, and I kept letting him know that. I guess I just wanted him to know someone was there for him. It was already hard to get a read on that dry farm boy when talking to him face to face, via text was a whole different challenge. I had no idea if I had helped the matter or made it worse, but I felt like it was what I needed to do. My mission was accomplished, my part complete, my duty done, I was finished where Jack Wayne was concerned, or so I thought.

That day had been busy and full of emotional chaos. There was also the chaos of the normal routines of work and getting kids to activities. In the midst of the world spinning faster than a tilt a whirl at a carnival, I had failed to fill Jason in on our newfound friendship. The girls had a basketball tournament that night, and I was meeting him at the game. I planned on sharing with him the events that had unfolded that day once we got home that night. Sometimes your plans have a mind of their own and don't go the way you had intended.

I made it to the game and engaged in my usual routine. I scoped out a seat and started climbing the bleachers in that unfamiliar gym. The smells of this gym were different than those at our home gym, but the faces were familiar and the anticipation of the farm boy's love story remained the same.   I sat next to Rachel, Mike sat on the other side of her. The awkwardness in the air was so thick it was almost like a stench was in the room. I knew that Jack still loved Rachel. Jack now knew that Rachel loved him back.   The three of us sat there not knowing where to go from here and walking among those who had no idea that their lives would soon be forever changed.

My heart skipped a quick beat when I caught a glimpse of my sweet husband. There he stood at the bottom of those bleachers peeking out from beneath his Rush Springs Redskins ball cap. He smiled and the light in his eyes made me a bit envious. In his ignorance, he was free of the heavy stench that was suffocating the rest of us. As Jason stood and contemplated how to make his way up to where we were sitting, Jack brushed right past him and made his way up the bleachers to plant himself right in front of me. He was far enough away from Rachel to not look extremely obvious to those oblivious of the recent confession, but close enough to make those of us that knew of the recent confession a little uncomfortable. I was certain that when Jack sat down on that bleacher, the temperature in the room increased about 20 degrees. I felt my ears begin to get hot and sweat beading up on the back of my neck. Jason finally made his way up to sit next to me, closest to the side Jack was on, and just when I thought the weight of the stench couldn't get any heavier, Jack reached over Jason, fist bumped me, and then patted Jason's leg and said, "Hey, man." Jason looked at me with a lost look, and reluctantly responded to Jack, "Hey, man." He turned away from Jack, looked at me with raised eye brows and a look of disgust. I was quickly reminded that Jason was in the dark about all that had unfolded today. Now the beads of sweat were rolling down my neck and my ears felt like they were on fire. I couldn't wait for that game to be over so I could get to the car and unload the weight I was carrying on to Jason. I could shed light onto this situation for him. The pressure of this tension, that I felt like was going to crush my body, would soon be relieved.

Jack chatted it up with everyone around us and made several comments to all of us, like nothing had ever happened. His wife was down on the gym floor, coaching our girls' basketball game. I didn't know how the man was doing it. I felt like everyone in the gym that night knew that these two loved each other, I mean I felt like he would have tried to be more discreet. Jack choosing to not sit so close to us would have been a great idea. Trying not to chat us up the whole game while his wife sat on the bench about four bleachers below us, that would have been another great idea. This game felt like it lasted for an eternity. Finally, the buzzer rang indicating the game was over, and hopefully some of my torment was over, as well.

Jason and I quickly walked to the dimly lit parking lot. We barely got the glass doors open as we stepped foot on the blacktop when Jason looked at me and said, "What was up with that guy? He just hit me on the leg like we are friends or something, I don't even like him, who does he think he is?" I tried to cut him off before he continued digging a bigger hole. "Well, I kind of sent him a text today?" I said with a big, over exaggerated smile, while I shrugged my shoulders in complete childlike innocence. "What do you mean, you sent him a text today?" Jason questioned in a very inquisitive and almost disgusted tone.

I was trying to figure out how to explain that I had not only sent Jack Wayne a text that day, but that I had opened the door of a potential friendship for the two of them. I felt like I was talking so fast, trying to fill him in on all of the events of the day, then I finally said it, "Oh, and I told him to call you if he needs someone to talk to," I shrugged again, in innocence, feeling somehow that would make the news go over better. "Why would you do that? That guy is an arrogant jerk. He walks around here like....." he paused trying to find the appropriate way to say some inappropriate things, and I just came busting through his thought process with my declaration of defense, "He's not an arrogant jerk, he's a broken man who wants his family back but is in a really tough spot and he needs people he can talk to. Considering I am not a dude, I felt like it would be better for me to offer your ear instead of mine." He sighed, knowing I was right, and then responded to me, "It's just none of our business. I don't even know how to help him." I quickly replied back, "I don't know either, but I know they just need someone to walk with them through this, whatever it looks like."

We got in our cars and I followed Jason's tail lights down that old back road leading us home. The girls chose to ride back with Jason that night, so I rode alone and replayed the last conversation that Jason and I had just finished up over and over in my head. I was defending him, this man that I barely knew. The tall rugged faced man that stood in doorway with that old dirty ball cap, that just a few months ago I also thought was an arrogant jerk. I had seen his heart, I was sad for him, I was bearing his burden, and with a fist bump that night a bond was created. In the moment of the madness and the panic, I had missed it. After further review, I was realizing what had happened. That bump was a reach out, a yes I need someone. So many times in life I had missed things that God had put right before me, and I had been lost in the chaos of life and the busyness, that I had never thought to put what had happened under further review. Thankfully tonight, I reviewed the play again, and realized that I had missed something. That night in the unfamiliar gym, under the stench of the confession and the chaos of the circumstance, a friendship was born, a bond was created, and I would soon realize that my life, too, would never be the same.

It had now been a few days since that panicked conversation in the parking lot of the old gym. Jason had asked me almost every day since that night if I had talked to the farm boy. There had been days that I had spoken to him, and days that had passed and I wouldn't. I had been married to Jason for almost fifteen years, so when he walked into the back door and asked, "Hey would you ask Jack if he has any land I can hunt on?" I knew that was his way of reaching out to Jack without coming out and saying he was reaching out to Jack. This inquiry had nothing to do with hunting for pigs, and everything to do with hunting to see if this "arrogant jerk" Jack Wayne was making it ok. I actually thought it was sweet, and at the same time comical.

I text Jack, "Hey, Jason is wanting to know if you have any land he can hunt pigs on?" Jack quickly responded, "Yes." I hollered at Jason from the kitchen, "Jack said yes." "Okay, ask him when I can come and check the places out," Jason hollered back from the laundry room. "Oh my gosh, can't you just text him yourself?" I asked impatiently. "No, just ask him," he said laughing. So I continued to be the middle man and asked Jack. He answered and told me later that afternoon would be fine.

Jason and I headed outside to do chores. Neither one of us had many words, I think we were both wrestling with all that was going on with them inside our own hearts and minds. We began cleaning out the chicken coop, and all of the sudden Jason picked up his rake and folding his calloused hands on top of it, he leaned his chin to rest on the top of them. He sighed and said, "Man, I hope he doesn't say anything to me about all of this, I don't even know what to tell him." It was eating him up. He knew that all of this mess would be a topic of conversation and he didn't know what to tell Jack to do. This man was standing at a fork in the road on his journey in life. On one path stood a woman that he had loved since he was twenty years old, she was the mother to his two beautiful daughters, the woman that held his heart, there were pieces of his soul woven into hers. On the other path stood a woman he had just married two years ago, she was a great friend to him, she had just given him a son, his only son, he was just a few months old. How does a man choose which path to take?

Jason and I stood there looking at each other when Jack's text came through, "Tell Jason I'm at the house when he is ready to check out these spots." I relayed the message to Jason and I could tell he was nervous. Comic relief is about my only coping skill in life, so I light heartedly said, "Seriously that guy doesn't even talk to the people he does know. I am sure he won't even mention it to you." He seemed somewhat relieved and headed out of the driveway and south to Jack's house.

A few hours had passed, I had continued working out in the

yard enjoying the beautiful spring day, I hadn't even noticed how much time had passed since Jason had left. He pulled into the driveway and I was excited to see how his day trip went with Jack. As soon as he stepped out of the truck, his eyes were stretched wide open, he smiled and said, "Well, I went to find a hunting place and I turned into Dr. Phil!" I honestly couldn't believe it, I said, "No way!! That super quiet guy that doesn't even know you, spilled his guts?" "Oh yeah girl. That guy has it bad. I was trying to avoid the topic, and he just straight called me out and said, "Don't sit over there like you don't know anything," what was I supposed to say to that? I almost jumped out of the truck!" I couldn't contain the laughter, so I just let it all out, cracking up. Jason's eyes got so big and he asked, "Are you seriously laughing right now? It was horrible, and this is not a laughing matter." The corner of his mouth cracked a smile. I composed myself, tried to silence my laughter, and managed to ask, "Well, what did you say to that?" He said, "I told him I didn't know much and then he just spilled it. He told me that he didn't care about anything in life right now, it is almost like he is just numb. Knowing that she loves him back and wants him is all that he can think about right now. He said he was willing to give everything he had up for her, just to be with her again. He doesn't want to lay another night in bed just thinking about her, he wants to actually get to hold her in his arms again. Girl, I'm telling you the dude has it bad, and he doesn't care who knows, and I'm pretty sure he is willing to do

63

anything just to have her back again." I, of course, followed all of this up with what would soon become the million dollar question, "So now what is the plan?" Jason turned away and began walking away, he shrugged his shoulders, shook his head, and said, "I don't think there is one."

6

In the Dark

The sun would rise the next day, and with it the burden of this mess was still among us. I heard the engine of a vehicle pull up in the driveway and the echo of a car door shutting. I peeked out to see Rachel making her way to the door. I met her in the driveway and she was sobbing. I said, "Did you talk to Mike?" She just shook her head affirming that she had. I said, "Oh no, was it that bad?" She just stood shaking her head back and forth, "No, it wasn't bad at all!" she managed to get out in between her sobs. I was so relieved, and somewhat proud of myself for suggesting the truth, I said, "See I told you the truth would set you free!!" She responded quickly, "He was so nice about it, and told me he understood how I would still have feelings for Jack after being married for so long and having children, and he just wanted me to be happy! But he wants to fight for me!" I honestly was at a loss for words. She continued on, "How do you turn your back on someone when they extend that kind of grace to you? Please tell me how I do that." There was extreme desperation in her voice as she pleaded with me. I unfortunately, once again, didn't have the answers she was looking for, I didn't have any answers. I couldn't imagine how helpless they felt. I could barely bare the weight of my own helplessness as just a spectator on this journey! We stood in the driveway hugging, crying, and I felt like I was squeezing her so hard, trying to hold the pieces of her heart together.

The hardest part, to me, of any crisis, is that while you are in the middle of a raging storm, life continues to go on all around you. You still have to go to work, you still have to be a mom, you still have to get up, get dressed, and live. So as life continued to go on, the days kept passing. There was still no plan, no direction, and no idea what each day would bring. It had been about three days since we stood in my driveway, me trying to hold the pieces of Rachel's life together, a physical representation of an emotional act I felt like I was juggling. On this day, it would all change. This day brought Jack

Wayne across Rachel's path at the calf barn. Rachel was at the barn helping Baylee with her show calf, Lolly. The sound of that old diesel feed truck interrupted the conversation between Rachel and Baylee. The truck pulled right up to the old barn, the diesel engine sound echoed throughout the pasture, and in an instant was quieted as Jack turned the truck off. The creaking sound of the door as it opened was almost like the announcement of his arrival. He stepped out of the feed truck and as his boot hit the gravel of that old road, Rachel's heart was racing like she was a teenage girl all over again. "Baylee, why don't you go down and see if KK needs help getting dinner ready," Rachel suggested. Baylee kind of looked at Rachel with a funny inquisitive look. Rachel made eye contact with her, raised her eyebrows, and nodded her on to KK's.

Baylee disappeared over the hill to KK's house and Jack made his way closer to Rachel and said, "Well, I've been doing a lot of thinking and praying, and I've been listening to a lot of sermons. On Sunday, I heard a great sermon and I felt like God told me that everyone gets a mulligan. You know in golf, it's a do over, everyone gets a do over." Rachel knew exactly what Jack was implying, he was telling this story with excitement in his voice and anticipation. For the farm boy, any kind of emotion in a conversation warranted that there must be something big about to happen. That beautiful, sun kissed, small town girl stood in the doorway of the barn with the sun reflecting off of her beautiful blonde hair, thankful for sunglasses because they were hiding the tears beginning to well up in her eyes. Jack continued to talk, Rachel was lost in her own thoughts. Every day for the past three years she would have given anything to hear those words come out of his mouth, but today was different. She didn't know what to do. She didn't know how she was going to hurt Mike, she didn't know how to turn her back on his grace and she stood now not knowing how to break Jack's heart all over again. Her hesitation was enough to do the job; she didn't need words to break his heart. Which was no surprise, their love story had survived the last three years without a word, and now it could die without a word.

The next morning my phone sounded like a kid with a BB gun trying to shoot birds out of a tree. Ding, ding, ding. I walked quickly to the phone. Jack Wayne's name came across the screen and I opened the text message to read, "Well, I appreciate your prayers, but I'm pretty sure I heard the words I needed to hear from her yesterday. We probably just don't need to talk anymore except about the girls. I love her very much, but we both have spouses and I guess we should just be happy with that. Maybe this is just what is best for now!" The harsh truth was raging in every word of that text message.

The truth was that Jack loved Rachel deeply and always would, but he couldn't trust her. He wanted to, but the brokenness of his heart and the fear of vulnerability crept in. His heart was fragile and still broken, held together with the band-aids of denial, lies, and pain. He feared what letting her love in would look like. There was a part of him that knew that letting her in was the only way for his heart to be whole again, it was ripping off those band aids that paralyzed him and put him in a place of uncertainty and extreme pain. He bore the pain of the heartbreak he would create for Alivia; she had been the one who put those band aids on his heart to begin with. She was there the nights he was heartbroken about the love he had lost with Rachel. She listened to his pain, she walked the road with him, she had accepted that he would never love her the way he loved Rachel, and she had embraced him, and more importantly loved him in the shape he was in. How would he just walk away from that kind of love himself? There would be the separation from his son that he knew would be inevitable if he followed his heart, and the pain of letting the walls crash down and letting the power of Rachel's love possess his heart once again.

I refrained from throwing all of that up on the poor guy and I dug deep and responded with a bunch of stuff about how I didn't know the answers for them, I wasn't Jesus, and I couldn't get in the hot seat with Jesus for them or I would. I would be lying if I said I wasn't a little sad. I didn't tell Jack that, I just ended the text with, "I'm sorry that was a lot of information, I am just trying to help but feel very helpless." He responded and said, "Well, I appreciate it but

I kinda feel the same way!"

We all wallowed in our helplessness, as Rachel wrestled in her uncertainty. She continued to wrestle and Jack was reading that uncertainty as rejection. Just a few hours later she text me, "I feel so selfish for telling Jack how I felt. Maybe I shouldn't have told him." What she didn't realize is that the enormity of her love for Jack took the choice away from her. As the pain of her secret continued to grow over the years, the power to keep it locked away no longer belonged to her.

There wasn't as much of an emotional attachment for me to the situation as there was for her. I could see that she had already made her decision. She had actually made her decision years ago. As soon as she had gotten remarried, that first Christmas she spent away from her family, her heart ached for her farm boy, and for her girls to be one again. That December day, although the weather was cold, the humility and the hurt she felt began to melt her heart of stone, and she began to allow truth back into her life. That day she had already decided what she wanted, she just wasn't sure if she would get what she wanted in this lifetime. She also was unsure if she could pay the price to get what she wanted. She felt like it was too late, too messy, and there was too much hurt. Those feelings clouded her mind. Not only was she sure what she wanted, she knew she couldn't live much longer without Jack.

We continued meeting at the track, and with every lap around that small town football field, another layer of pain from the past was peeled back. I could see the struggle and hear all of those thoughts wrestling her down and wearing her out. It was another day of walking, another lap, the same conversation. Today would be different though, as she was talking and talking and talking, in circles I could feel the words beginning to form and they were just right there on the tip of my tongue. I couldn't take another lap of the same conversation and the same problem and no solution. Finally, she stopped talking for just a moment and without one second of hesitation, I blurted out, "Ok girl, if you are staying with Mike, then you are done talking to Jack. You are going to have to go through Alivia to discuss the girls, and you are going to have to just separate yourself from him. Talking to him and not being with him is just too hard for you." Her head spun around so fast I think I felt a small breeze of wind, and with extreme sternness in her voice, she stopped the tears, looked me straight in the face and she said, "No, there is no way I can do that, I can't live without him." In that moment I pushed her to say out loud what we both already knew. She had made up her mind, she just wanted to continue to believe the lies that her head was telling her heart, because in that place where she was lying to herself, there was less pain than the place she was headed when she would step out of the darkness of the lies and into the sunshine of the truth.

That step for all of us, no matter our circumstance, is always scary, but necessary for true healing. When we keep ourselves trapped in the darkness of lies and denial, there is no growth and death is creeping upon us. When we step out of the lies and step into the light of the truth, we can grow, we can heal, and ultimately we can be restored.

With every sunrise, the moment our eyes would open and our mind would waken from our slumber, although we were all under different roofs, our minds were on the same page. The same questions flooded all of our minds, *"Would restoration come today? Would they get back together? Had they decided to stay locked away in their prison of pretending?"* When I would drop the girls off at school, I would pass KK's classroom, I would always stick my head in the door and every day it was the same question, "Any news?" I would typically shrug and then look to her, wondering the same thing. Had she talked to Jack? She was wondering what I was getting from Rachel, we were all in turmoil with them. They didn't even know the answers, I'm not sure why we were expecting resolve. We all just seemed to spin around in the unknown.

7

For Such a Time as This

The school year was coming to an end. It had now been a couple of months since Rachel drove into my driveway and spoke those three life changing words, "I told him." All the chaos and the unknown was still there lingering. I was trying to keep myself busy, but distraction was at every event, every moment my eyes were open my mind was on this mess. It was track season for the girls and it was now in full swing. This activity landed Rachel and I a lot more time together. It happened to be the morning of a track meet, we were meeting up to ride together. I had talked with Jack a few times over text about what had been going on and he seemed pretty confident in his decision, he was going to figure out how to get back with Rachel. Even if Rachel had decided to stay with Mike at this point, the damage of the confession and the emotions that raged from that moment had already littered Jack Wayne's world and no matter what happened from here, he would never be the same.

The entire drive for me to go and meet Rachel, I began thinking of all that was at stake. Mike's life would forever be changed and he would forever be scarred. Alivia would now raise her son by herself, and lose the father of her child, someone she had chosen, who she seemed to love. It just didn't seem fair. No matter what direction he went, he would lose. I guess all of this had been spinning in my head and weighing on my heart, and as I walked into Rachel's house to catch a ride with her, something just came over me. She was doing her best at pretending that all was well, and she was happy, and everything was fine, but it wasn't. The problem was that she had been pretending so long, it was a normal for her, a familiar path, she was so good at it, and at times I think she fooled herself.

That day she was standing at the bar in her kitchen. She was packing an ice chest for the girls and putting things in her bag. I was just staring at her. She stopped and looked at me, laughed, and said, "What?" I said, "You can't stay here! You can't keep doing this! Or maybe you can. Maybe this is what you want, but if it is, and you are not going home to Jack, you have to tell him. You have to tell him now. Do not let him leave his baby, and his wife, and then change your mind. If you can't do it then your gonna have to tell him now!" I was crying, and I felt horrible after the words had left my mouth, but at the same time I felt better. I didn't sugar coat those words. They were hard to speak, but when I finally got up enough nerve to speak them, I said them with conviction, without any fear of what she was going to think, and I said it almost protectively.

I don't know what had happened, that fist bump, and a few texts between Jack and I, and I could see his hurt and his pain. Most importantly, for a small moment during this season I had seen his heart. It was battered and torn and broken, but it was still beating. It was beating with the hope that she was coming home to him. We just stood in that kitchen and cried, and looked at each other for a few very awkward moments. She finally broke the silence and said, "I know!" We hugged for what felt like a long time and held each other extremely tight. With the release of our grip, we walked out the door, and didn't mention the conversation again. We tried to just be in those moments with the girls, but the thought of their circumstance was never far from our minds.

Days continued to pass and we were all still spinning in their uncertainty. That spinning soon came to a screeching halt just a few weeks after our last track meet. I woke up early that morning and started making my way to the bathroom. Jason passed me in the hall with one eye open and asked, "Did you see the text from Rachel this morning?" I barely had my own eyes open and said, "No, I literally just woke up, what's up?" He said, "I don't know she just said, "Pray for me friends, I'm walking on water today!" It took us both a minute for it to register and then we both gasped, "Oh my gosh, she's doing it today!" I said. I skipped the bathroom and headed to the kitchen where my phone was plugged in. I begin typing faster than I had ever composed a text before. After several texts back and forth I had confirmed what we had suspected, she was packing up her things and heading out of her house today. I was swamped at work and couldn't leave. I wanted so badly to go and help her. Although I wasn't physically with her, my heart and mind were with her all day. While Mike was at work, she frantically spent the nest few hours packing up her things and putting them into her jeep. Once she was all loaded up, she made the painful drive to her parent's house.

A few hours later she sent a text and said, "Can you help me tell the girls?" "Sure," I said, "just tell me when and where!" She replied, "The girls get out of piano at 4:30, I'll be at KK's." "Ok I will be there!" I replied. My heart was racing, I was nervous, I didn't know how I was going to help, or what I could even say, but I was going. I pulled into KK's driveway, back behind the protection of the trees, and Jack's truck was there. My heart sank and I thought to myself, *"Ok, Jack decided to come and help her, I will text her and tell her I will chat with her later."* I began typing the text, keeping my foot on the brake. As soon as I pressed send, I was going to throw that truck in reverse and head home. Before I got the first sentence typed, a knock on my window startled me. I jumped and fumbled my phone a bit. I turned my head to see who was at the window and there stood Jack with a smile on his face! This was not a time I thought a smile would be worn, so confused, I rolled my window down. "Kill it," he said, still smiling. "What?" I questioned. "Kill it and come inside, you know turn it off!" he responded with his one raised eyebrow, a smirk, and a sarcastic tone, speaking to me like I was the dumbest person on the planet.

I think I was still in shock for many reasons. I was in shock he was there, I was in shock that this dry, no personality man, felt it appropriate to make a joke, in a time like this. I reluctantly turned the truck off, hopped out of the pick-up and began to follow Jack up to KK's door. Before we reached the door I said, "Sorry, I was so confused, Rachel asked me to come and help her tell the girls she had moved out of her house. I didn't expect to see you here." He is still wearing that smirk and responds, "Well, they are my kids!" Still raising his eyebrows at me and shaking his head, continuing to talk to me like I was the dumbest person on the planet. "Oh, I'm aware of whose kids they are, I am just shocked you are here," I responded, reciprocating his tone right back to him.

I walked into KKs house and was refraining from many words. I wasn't sure what they were telling the girls. Were they just telling them that Rachel was leaving Mike, or that they were getting back together? I had no idea. When I walked around that doorway and saw the look on Baylee's face, I no longer stood in the dark. She sat at the sacred table swinging those long legs and smiling from ear to ear. They had told them the truth, that they were going to be getting back together. I sat down at the table next to Rachel, she had been crying, probably all day. Her eyes were red and swollen, and she hugged me, we exchanged a kiss on the cheek. There was a sense of relief, but it wasn't much. There were still so many turns before they got back on the road that would lead them back home to each other. We all sat at the table at KK's with a spirit of celebration, but also with the dreaded reality that hung over us. The hardest part of this journey had not even begun. I wondered if telling the girls before they even began this journey would end up being a death trap for Jack. That was something only time would tell.

Jack and Rachel had gone on a tragic detour. When their marriage got rough, and their hearts were hardened, and Satan told them it was not salvageable, they chose to listen to that lie and they moved on without each other, they turned off the path that God had put them on. They came to a detour sign and Rachel decided she would turn one way, find love somewhere else, and work really hard at pretending she was happy. This act she put on helped distract her and it helped her ease the pain her pride caused. She wanted Jack to think she didn't love him and she sure didn't need him. He sat back and watched for a while, and after believing the act of happiness that Rachel was putting on, he left his road and turned off. He, too, found love somewhere else, and now had a child.

Satan wants us to believe that a detour is our only option. In our society we are not waiters. We are drive thru generation junkies. We want instant gratification, but what we fail to recognize is that although the gratification is instant, the regret is forever. Jack and Rachel had chosen to not wait on their road to be repaired. They chose not to work with God to restore their marriage, or their family, they decided to believe the lie that the detour was the only option. Now the detour had led them on a very destructive path that would cause so much more heartache and pain than they would have had to experience had they been patient while God was repairing their hearts.

Now that Rachel had told Mike everything and had moved out, the elephant in the room was everyone wondering, "When would Jack leave? When would he tell Alivia?" Jack had a plan. He decided it would be best to wait and tell Alivia when the school year was over. It was just a couple of weeks away, so Jason and I tried to keep Rachel busy, and we walked as closely with Jack as we possibly could as he wrestled with the words and the timing to tell Alivia that her life would never be the same again. Although it was only about seventeen days from the day Rachel left until the end of school, those just might have been the longest seventeen days of our lives.

Once Rachel had ripped off the band-aid she had been wearing, packed up her bags, and left the driveway she used to call her own, the conversations between her and Jack became more frequent. I could see the pressure caving in on them. They were raging to touch again, a simple brush of the hand, or even just a peck on the cheek. They wanted to hold each other, to comfort each other, to be reunited.

I had seen the way they looked at each other lately. Before the confession, when he was just the farm boy in the doorway, I thought their love story was loud. The confession had ignited that love story to a full blown tornado siren. My heart was so heavy for them. A part of Rachel was free, but yet she was still unsure Jack would be able to leave Alivia. Jack was so weighted by the misery and the pain, he was now carrying it around on his face, in his posture. He was not a malicious man, Alivia was his friend, a great friend, and reality was she was his wife. He didn't want to hurt her, and I believe he loved her, but his heart was with Rachel. The exhaustion of having no right answer was taking its toll on all of us.

Rachel and I had been together all weekend with the girls. Sunday afternoon the girls had a band concert at the school. Jason and I walked in with Rachel and all of our girls, found our seats, and enjoyed the concert. Out of the corner of my eye, I could see Jack sitting with KK and Pops a few rows back. That awkward stench was in the room again. The concert ended, and the girls got their bags out of Rachel's car to head back to Jack's old, white farm truck. We all hugged Rachel bye and headed to the diner in town.

We had walked in with Rachel and the girls, and we would walk out with Jack and the girls. I couldn't imagine how the girls felt. They weren't even my parents and I longed to be able to be at the dinner table with both of them at the same time. I longed for all of us to sit together at the concert and not be forced to pretend to be strangers.

As we sat at the diner, Jack tried to tease and make small talk, despite his efforts the conversation always found its way back to, "When are you going to tell Alivia?" That day, with the sun shining through those diner windows, it almost made the darkness he carried overshadow his face. He lowered his voice, as everyone in the diner knew him, and in almost a whisper he leaned down and said, "I want to tell her, but her dad is having a big surgery next week and I don't want her to have to bear this burden, too."

Who was this man, and was he being for real right now? I thought it was incredibly sweet and caring of him to be so sensitive, and not want Alivia to bear this burden. At the same time, I felt compelled to share with him, "Brother, you know there is never going to be a right time, right?" I questioned, as I leaned closer to him, raising my own eyebrows. He looked at me with a deer in the headlights look, but tried to confidently answer me, "Well, I know." With the lost look on his face, I knew he didn't know. I don't think he realized that it would never be the right time to tell a woman that her world is crashing down around her. It's never a good time to tell a woman that the father of her very new baby boy, is in love with another woman, and always has been. It will never be a good time to share that the relationship that you have with someone, was built through the pain of your past. That the friendship that you now have that means everything to her, was just a friendship for a stormy season for you, and you needed her to carry the umbrella so you could make it through. The love that she knew for him which was strong and genuine and unconditional was not reciprocated on his end. His vow and his promise was about to come to an end. For this, there is never a good time!

8

The Web We Weave

Over the past several months of walking this uncertain road, this incredible relationship had developed between Jack and I. Although not romantic in any way, it was powerful and rare. There was a love and bond that we knew we would always be there for each other. It was like I had found that brother I had always wanted. Although not connected by our parents' blood, or DNA, we were connected by a much more powerful blood, the blood of Christ.

Jesus had allowed our paths to cross. As this situation began to unfold, I thought that God allowed our paths to cross because he needed us, but what I would later learn is I needed him just as much as he needed me. This bond created an unspoken guarantee, we would finish our race in life together. No matter what kind of curveball life would throw our way or how beat up we would get, there was an unspoken certainty that we would fight the battles, and celebrate the victories side by side.

The relationships between all of us strengthened and a sense of understanding began to develop in my own heart. I didn't blame Alivia or Rachel for wanting to fight for Jack. I now knew what it was like to need Jack Wayne in your life. He loved in a way that was pure, genuine, and transparent. The way he loved was silent, yet strong, and consistent. His love wasn't based on performance, if he loved you, it was just because, it wasn't a love you could earn. It was a love that rescued, a love that gave hope and life. I had lived in a prison of performance love my entire life. I had never learned how to accept unconditional love, especially from men. My dad and I had a strained relationship, well, all of my dad's relationships were strained. Although I had gained much healing in my life through the relationship with my husband, there was still this void, a piece of me that needed that male love, acceptance, and affection. There was a part of me that longed for that fatherly/brotherly love of protection and just true acceptance. I had found that healing love in my relationship with Jack. There is power in finding something you never had, you realize just how much you have missed.

I imagined Alivia loading Avery up, strapping him in his car seat, and looking back at the place she had called home. Glancing back in her rearview mirror, knowing the life she thought she was building was fading as she continued to drive. These thoughts were agonizing. Being loved by Jack and his family was a rare gift. A gift that filled your lungs with life, a love that changed you for the better, and a love that only comes around once in a lifetime. How is it that you walk away from the comfort, security, and power of that kind of gift? The answer is simple, you don't walk away. You fight, and hold on as long as you can, until you wake up and realize that the person you're hanging on to, let go of you a long time ago; or the harsh realization that maybe they were never hanging on to you at all. Jack and Alivia had a relationship, but Jack and Rachel had something else, something more. I believe Jack loved Alivia, but there was something so powerful he had with Rachel, he couldn't even explain it himself.

The power of whatever it was that pushed Jack to Rachel was about to shatter through Alivia's world just as soon as Jack could figure out how to get the right words out of his mouth. What made this web even harder to untangle was that Alivia had not done anything wrong. She had always taken good care of Jack, and loved him in a way that he was unable to reciprocate. What I think he was missing in his pursuit of Rachel, is that it was Alivia's love that had brought healing to his life when he was broken before. The rage and the power of Rachel's love was definitely drawing him in, but he had forgotten how that love had shattered him before. His ability to love now was because he had the steady love of Alivia for the past two years. The man just continued to be in a tough place, there was no right answer. Although he was physically present with Alivia he, like Rachel, was missing a piece of himself, a part of his heart.

That day at the diner was a Sunday, and in just three short days Alivia would head out of town for her dad's surgery. Jack continued to wrestle with his heart and his mind, he was exhausted. He was trying to find the words to tell Alivia that his heart had never belonged to her. He was so broken thinking about hurting her and losing Avery, but at the same time living without Rachel left a void in his life so loud he couldn't possibly continue life without her. This turmoil that tore his heart in two different directions was creating a sense of suffering in Jack's soul that he couldn't bear much longer. The immensity of his pain was engulfing his existence. Thursday morning, once Alivia was out of town, there was a small glimpse of relief for Jack. For the next few days he didn't have to go home and pretend, he didn't have to face the pressure of what he was going to say to her, for the next few days he would just get to be Jack.

It was late that Friday night, and the girls had made lots of plans together for the weekend celebrating that their last day of school was on Thursday. They were ringing in the summer with sleepovers, campfires, and S'mores at KK's house, oh the magic of childhood. The school year ending was cause for all of us to celebrate, even the parents. The end of the year activities are every day and exhausting. Jason and I had been finishing up some errands and decided since the girls would be with KK for the evening we would celebrate the end of bedtimes, early mornings, and lunch packing with some dinner. We ate at one of our favorite Mexican food places and then began to drive home. It was just a sense of relief to know summer was finally here. The moon was big and lighting up the sky that night, the air was crisp, I had the window down a bit, the music up, just Jason and I sitting in each other's presence in the truck. For a brief moment, the turmoil we had all been in seemed to have disappeared. The music was singing to my soul and all distractions were out. That old highway was vacant that night, and it really was like it was just us and the world. It felt nice and peaceful, almost too good to be true.

We were just about five miles from home when my freedom from the turmoil quickly ended. A text from KK came through saying they needed prayers for Alivia's dad, he wasn't doing well at all. Before I could even respond, Rachel called me. She said Jack was in bad shape and she wanted me to check on him. She was limited to what she could do for him, as they were trying to be respectful and not be together until their divorces were filed and Alivia had been told of their plan. Before I even hung up Jack was texting me, "Are y'all coming up?" The next statement that came through the phone pierced my heart as I read the words, "I need you!" This tall, rugged man, who did not make a habit of showing emotion or vulnerability must have been in great emotional distress to type these words and press send.

I turned the radio down, tears were already streaming down my face, I rolled the window up so Jason could hear me, "We have to go to the cabin." Jason looked away from the road with his eyebrows squinted and said, "What? It's midnight, I'm headed...." he stopped mid-sentence as the street light lit up the tears that were streaming down my face. "What's wrong?" he asked, now with a different tone. "I don't really know. KK sent a text saying Alivia's dad wasn't doing well, Rachel called and said Jack was in bad shape, and Jack text and said he needed us." Jason returned his eyes to the road and said, "Tell him we are on our way." Before I could respond my phone died, but within just a few minutes we had pulled up to the dimly lit cabin, tucked away in the woods. When the crickets quieted themselves long enough, you could hear the small sound of fish jumping in and out of the water. There was a sense of peace out there under the blanket of stars, but there was a heaviness anticipating what we were about to hear. Although we had turned the car off and stepped out, the headlights were still beaming onto the porch of the cabin, and there he stood. The silhouette of the tall farm boy was there on that porch as he had been in that gym doorway so many months before. But this time he didn't stand with confidence or with a sense of wonder and love in his face, his posture was sad and he was broken.

I refrained myself from running, but I got to him as quickly as I could, Jason right behind me. I stood and hugged this man, who I had begun to love like a brother. As we embraced, tears streaming down my face, I was praying that for just a moment in time God would allow me to bear the pain he was carrying. We stood for a few minutes and just hugged. As I felt his chest quivering with each tear that fell from his face, my heart just ached. He did love this woman, and he loved what he had lost with Rachel. His highway was divided, but at some point, he was going to have to choose a direction and get to living. When we left the embrace I stepped into the cabin, Jason patted Jack and we all found a seat. Jack sat in the recliner, Jason and I sat on the couch across from him. We had only been there a few minutes when Rachel came through the door. She was just waiting for us to get there. She wanted to comfort Jack, but she didn't want to be there alone with him, in fear that their emotion would take over and they would wake up to regret, as they were trying to handle this situation with as much integrity as one can, in a circumstance such as this.

That night was absolutely heartbreaking. Jack had received word from Alivia that her dad had left this earth that big starry summer night in May. Jack was unsure how he would ever tell Alivia now. She would be bearing the burden of her father's death, and now he was going to tell her that she would be alone. He was so sad for her that night, I remember him saying, "I want to comfort her, but I want to comfort her as a friend, and not her husband, how do you do that?" I had no answers, as usual. I just sat crying as he shared his heart. We sat for a while in silence, all sad, the air so heavy. Then, piercing the silence, Rachel spoke up with tears staining her face and her voice impaired, "It's ok Jack, if you can't tell her, and you can't leave her, it's ok. I will be ok. I mean, I love you, and I want to be with you, and I should have never let you go. But if you can't do it, I'll be ok." Jack just cried, there was no declaration of love to Rachel, there was nothing, just tears all around. I had never seen a man in such confliction in my life.

There were moments that night, that through his reaction of the news of Alivia's dad, I saw that he did love her and cared about her. I saw through his desire to have Rachel there that he loved her as well. That night I wondered if Jack Wayne would ever be whole this side of heaven, or if he would forever live in confliction. I wondered at that point, if they hadn't told the girls, if he would just stay with Alivia. I wondered if Rachel hadn't already left Mike if they would have chalked this confession up to a simple act of closure and move forward with their lives. They had allowed their emotions to rage through and ignite actions that had already created a lot of damage, maybe irreparable damage. These were things only time would tell. The silence in the room was painful, we all just sat in this moment of sadness and mourned.

My heart would continue to stay in the shape it had been since I had been walking this road with these people, maybe it was its new permanent condition, broken. I didn't know what was going to happen. What would Rachel do now? Would she go back to Mike? Would she just be alone and yearn for this man that held her heart and had pieces of her soul? How would Jack keep going on pretending? Was he pretending? I mean I felt like he did love Alivia, just different than he loved Rachel? The fact that he was extremely torn was brought into the light that night with the news of Alivia's dad. Would Jack keep locking away the truth, embracing the death grip of the lies that had now woven such a big web? The girls were now involved, KK and Pop were involved, the web was bigger and with every passing day another silk added to it, making it almost impossible to know how to get out. This web of uncertainty, confession, and emotion would soon suffocate the life out of Jack if he didn't move fast.

We sat with Jack for several hours until the wee hours of the morning, then we left and headed home. I was physically sick, my stomach in as much distress as my heart. I tried to get some rest but after just a few hours decided to get up. I read, and prayed, and cried. KK text me and said she would be having dinner at her house that night for Jason and I and the girls, she figured Rachel would bring Baylee and Peyton. Jack would be at home, awaiting Alivia to return from out of town.

My heart was heavy all day. I sent Jack a text telling him I was praying, but didn't text much the rest of the day. I didn't know what to say, and honestly I was just so sick and sad that I wasn't up for much conversation myself. The evening finally came, the girls and I got dressed to head to KK's. Jason was going to be late, he was out working cattle. That night when I walked into KK's house, the magic that normally resided there seemed a bit dim. The mood was sad and heavy, and Rachel sat at the table facing the big window. She didn't even look my way as the door opened. I leaned over the back of her chair and put my arms around her shoulders. We both just wept. KK didn't have many words that night, which of course we all knew that was a rarity.

The girls and I had only been there a few minutes when that diesel truck sound began to echo in the house. Jack made his way up the driveway. He had decided to come for dinner as he anxiously awaited Alivia's return from Missouri. I couldn't imagine her agony as she sat for over five hours with the weight of the world literally on her shoulders. She was a daddy's girl. Her social media pages were full of pictures of her and her dad. He had been her softball coach growing up, they had spent many of hours together on and off the field, you could tell all of this from pictures. I can't imagine the void that occurs when you lose that important man in your life. My heart was sad for her, as well, and even sadder knowing she was coming home to this mess.

We all found our place at that long wooden table, staring out the picture window seeing that big moon shine in. It wasn't quite as magical as it usually was. Jack sat at one end, Rachel sat at the other, there were no words, but as usual, there was no need for words. His heart was bleeding, he was so torn, and there was so much pain. He wanted to hold her, to allow the power of her love to consume him in this very moment, and take away the pain. She longed to hold him and be the comfort that she knew he so badly needed. The sadness that he wore that night on his face was crippling. There were no tears streaming down his face, he even tried to crack a few jokes, but the majority of the night his face was somber, and when I locked eyes with him, even though it was for just a moment, I could feel the ache in his heart and the weight of the misery he had to bear. Jason caught a ride to KK's and finished up supper with us. Everyone was trying hard to make conversation, but the forced effort was evident.

Jack got the call that Alivia was almost home. As he left, my heart ached. We all stood on the porch as he walked alone to his truck. I wanted to go with him, I didn't want him to have to go home by himself. He never took his eyes off Rachel as he got into his truck, they were having another conversation without words, in a language that only their hearts could understand. The diesel truck echoed through the trees as he started it up, even the loud noise of that pick up couldn't drown out the sounds of our breaking hearts that night. I stood on the porch of KK and Pop's log cabin and watched until all I could see was his tail lights.

I left KK's with a knot in my stomach and an ache so deep in my heart it felt hard to breathe. Tears streamed down my face as we drove those dark, back country roads home. We lived just a few miles north of KK's house. Jason and I rode home in silence - no radio, no words, just a painful silence. Out of the silence, Jason's voice startled me, "Can you imagine having to go home tonight and just pretend?" Through all the pain and agony of this journey, I don't know that I had ever really stopped and truly asked that question. As I pondered the pain of pretending, my thoughts were all over the board. You know pretending when you are a kid, that's fun. I remember pretending to be a princess, or a teacher, or a doctor. For a few hours, I could be anything I wanted to be. As we grow up, pretending isn't as much fun as it used to be, it actually becomes painful. It's painful to pretend to love someone in a way that you really don't. It's painful to pretend to want to be somewhere when your heart is really somewhere else. Some people, they love to pretend, they love to be someone or something they aren't.

Jack Wayne wasn't a pretender. He didn't like pretending. His heart had always belonged to Rachel. He pretended that he had let her go, and moved on with Alivia. He pretended to love Alivia in a way that I'm not sure he really did, because reality was, he didn't have the capacity to love Alivia the way he needed to because his heart was occupied with that blue eyed, blonde beauty that he fell in love with so many years before. Just like when you are a kid, pretending comes to an end. When your done playing princess, the reality that you have to take off your heels, pick up your mess, and hang up your tiara, is there staring you in the face. Pretending as a grown up is no different. Pretending comes to an end eventually. Reality is waiting to knock you down.

Jack's reality was knocking; he was hesitant to quit pretending. I don't know that it was fear, but compassion, that held him in his painful state of pretending. Alivia's dad was gone, and Jack's heart ached for her and the loss of her dad. The compassion of Jack's heart was inspiring and left you in a sense of awe and almost unbelief. How could a man be such a good man, and have such a mess on his hands?

In an internal agony, I watched Jack wrestle with his decision and his emotions. He was kind hearted, and beneath his hard, dry, exterior, he was soft and tender. God began to show me a small glimpse of why he weighs the heart and not the actions of a man. I had the great privilege, in this situation, to not only know the actions of the man, but to also know his heart. I knew that his desire to be with Rachel and to put his family back together was not a desire that came from malicious motives. He agonized over hurting Alivia and losing Avery, but sat in misery not being with the woman he had always loved.

If someone would have told me the story of a man who got divorced, married another woman, had a child with this woman, then wanted to get back with his first wife, I would have been the first in line to throw the stones of judgment, but to see one's heart changes everything. Jack Wayne had a good heart, he had just experienced a bad season, and the consequences of that bad season were about to come crashing in on him.

9

Still In the Dark

It was a beautiful summer day. I approached the church, the parking lot was full of cars, lined all the way down the street. There were people standing outside. I slowly drove by. I even second guessed myself for attending. The thought crossed through my mind to keep driving, but I felt like I needed to be there for Jack and for the girls if they needed me. Jack knew I was there for him, although we had to act as strangers. I had text him the day before to let him know I would be there to support him and the girls, although I knew we wouldn't speak that day, and by the looks of things, we probably wouldn't even see each other, it was so packed. I finally found a place to park and made the long, lonely, painful walk up to the church door. There were a few seats left, but it was extremely full in there, they were bringing chairs in for those waiting outside. As I stepped up to sign the book, the man seating people approached me reverently "Just one?" he asked. "Yes sir," I answered. He nodded for me to follow him. We made our way up an aisle, and as we approached the front, my heart was racing. He stopped in front of a pew just two rows back from the front, and he pointed to the vacant space at the end of the pew.

The stage was covered in colorful summer flowers, and the music playing was a beautiful song describing our moments in heaven. Just a few minutes passed and the family was escorted in. As the men begin to lead them in, Alivia's mom, her sister, and Alivia made their way into the row that was right across the church from me. Behind them filed in Baylee, Peyton, and Jack. I briefly made eye contact with him, and then avoided eye contact the rest of the service. The service was absolutely beautiful; Alivia had done an incredible job honoring her Dad. As the service was coming to a close, Alivia stepped up to the podium to speak about her dad. She finished up her tribute by sharing some things her dad had taught her, like giving people chances, and she then followed that up with a declaration of love to Jack. Her words were piercing, like salt being poured in a wound. I tried not to look at Jack, but I couldn't help it. Baylee and I locked eyes first. We were having our own conversation now, without words. Jack never made eye contact with me, Alivia, or anyone else. As she declared her love for him, he kept his eyes on the floor, never to meet hers, and trying to hide from the pain that this moment was causing him.

The service had finally come to an end and I headed out alone. I stepped onto the gravel parking lot and began to make my walk to the car. I pulled out my phone and there was a text, "I got flowers today from Mike :(" Rachel said. I responded, "I just left a funeral with Jack and Alivia." Basically I was saying, I win, my day was worse!! The day continued on with miserable reminders of what a horrible situation this was. I called Rachel when I left the funeral. She was sobbing. She was sad for Alivia for losing her dad and sad for Mike, who was losing her. I don't know how they were doing it. If I were to be painfully honest with myself and anyone else, if I had to have walked one day in Rachel's shoes, I would have wanted to hate Alivia for sleeping with the man I loved, for having his child, and for now being the reason that kept us apart. I even made this statement to Rachel once, and her reply was, "It's my fault, not hers. If I wouldn't have left she wouldn't have had the chance to be with him." Blaming someone else is so much easier than accepting the blame yourself, but Rachel never placed that blame on Alivia. I could see why Jack's heart was conflicted.

I headed south to KK's to try and find some relief from the pain of the misery. When I pulled up Rachel and Baylee were in the back room. KK was in the kitchen, frazzled, and a bit upset. I didn't even think to ask KK what was wrong. I figured it was just the obvious, the weight of all of this that we carried together. She had been at Alivia's parents taking care of Avery during the service. She was unaware of the declaration of love from the pulpit, but it had been mentioned to her by the girls. She finally asked, in almost a whisper, "What did Alivia say to Jack at the funeral from the stage?" I shared that it was excruciating to hear and extremely sad, like pouring salt into an open, bleeding, heart, she stood and genuinely shared her love for this man and the kids. She said, "Well, that is why Baylee is so upset, she feels terrible." I could see why, we all felt terrible. The very bitter, cold, extremely harsh truth is, like the country song says, "You can't make a heart love somebody, you can lead a heart to love, but you can't make it fall." Alivia was kind and sweet, and you could tell that she genuinely loved Jack and she loved the girls. She was doing everything right, there was nothing else she could have done, she just wasn't his choice.

I walked down the hallway of KK's with a heavy heart, passing by the photo lined walls of Jack and his brother when they were kids. The light in Jack's eyes in those photos, before life had crushed him, it was vibrant and happy. I stood for a moment in that hallway reflecting on that fact; the things life throws at us, we must choose if it takes the life out of us, or we step up and swing for the fences turning a curve ball into a homerun. I was sure hoping Jack would step up to the plate, but I wasn't sure how he would turn this mess into a score in his favor. It seemed to be an inevitable strike out. I was scrambling trying to gather the words to say to Baylee, and realized standing in the hallway of memory lane wasn't going to make this any easier. I opened the door to KK's room and Baylee was standing in front of the mirror, tear stained, red eyes, as Rachel stood behind her, running her fingers through Baylee's long blonde hair and trying to comfort her. I walked across the room, leaned against the vanity that Baylee was standing in front of and simply asked, "What's going on, babe?" She didn't say anything, she just shrugged, as she blinked back more tears. Rachel tilted her head sideways and leaned down to Baylee, and said, "It's okay to be sad for Alivia about her Dad." Baylee just continued to break down. I hugged her and asked, "Is that what's bothering you?" She just looked up at me with those tear stained eyes.

Loyalty is hard to understand, even as an adult. What I gathered in just those few moments was that Baylee's allegiance ultimately lied with her daddy, but her heart was broken for Alivia. Now that she knew her mom and dad were getting back together, she wasn't sure if feeling sad for Alivia was permissible. I myself was in the same battle. I felt very sad for Alivia and her sweet baby boy Avery. They would walk away from this mess with the most heartache and the most damage done, with the least amount of responsibility for what had happened. I, too, was like Baylee. My loyalty lied with Jack. We had walked this painful path together. He had been a part of my healing, and me a part of his. I felt I would forever be bonded to him, but I still felt a strong sadness for Alivia and all the pain that was headed her way. I hugged Baylee for just a few seconds, then asked her, "Are you mad at Dad?" She quickly shook her head no. "Are you mad at Mom?" She again shook her head no. "Well, here's the deal. Dad cares about Alivia, and Dad doesn't want to hurt her, but he loves Mom. It's okay for you to care about Alivia, too, and it's okay to be sad for her, and it's okay to be confused, or mad, or whatever you're feeling. What's important is that you talk through your feelings with Dad and Mom." She shook her head in agreement with me, hugged me, and we walked out. I wished someone was asking me to talk about my feelings. I, too, felt sad and confused and had no idea how this all was going to unfold at this point.

Jack's heart was torn completely in two different directions; how would he ever choose what to do? Well, the choice had already been made, but would he have the courage to make his choice a reality? His choice had been made the day Rachel walked out his door three years ago. He never wanted the divorce. He wanted to be back with her, but now there were so many complications, so many other lives involved. The prison they were now locked in almost seemed worse than before. Before the confession, they both knew they loved each other, but they had not expressed those feelings to each other, therefore they both stood in the dark as to what the other one felt. Now that the power of the confession had consumed their souls and their hearts, they were in a constant battle with their minds as to what the right decision would be. Do you go home and break the hearts of your new spouses and tear up another family, or do you lie in bed every night next to your spouse, longing for the person who holds your heart? There were no answers. There was no reaction to this situation that would bring resolve. There was no solution. Where would they go from here?

That question lingered and haunted us all. It was just a few days after Alivia's dad's funeral, and Jason and I and our girls had a big trip planned. We would be leaving out of town for seven days. We actually would be out of the country. There would be no phone service and no checking in. I would be in the dark for the next seven days. Which, honestly, even though I was in the country, even in the same town with them, I guess reality was, we were all in the dark.

10

A Highway Divided

We loaded up our luggage and waved goodbye to Rachel standing in our driveway. She had been staying with us some since she had moved out. It was hard leaving her there. We sat in the car, together as a family, waving goodbye, and she stood there alone. She would walk into the house that night alone, and she would lay there and wonder if alone would become her new companion. I had to work hard to be present on that trip. Although we were thousands of miles from home, in the middle of the ocean, with each sunrise and sunset the Lord and I chatted much about my friends, who had become my family, and my heart was still at home. When our boat finally ported, after our seven-day adventure, the hot summer sun beat down on us and I had to squint to find my way back to the truck. My heart was racing in anticipation to hear what all could have happened in those seven days while we were away. Had Jack told Alivia that he still loved Rachel? Had Jack decided to stay with Alivia and not lose Avery? What awaited me when I held down that power button on my phone? Would there be sadness and the reality of the prison they were still locked in, or would the truth have finally set them both free, and would they be making their way down the road to restoration, toward each other, one step closer to home? The questions swarmed around in my head like bees around a hive. I finally got the phone turned on and settled into the truck for the ride home.

I began texting everyone letting them know we were back. Rachel informed me that Jack had sent her to Florida to spend some time with her friend, she wouldn't be making it back home for a few more days. I assumed with this response that Jack had sent her out of town knowing that when he told Alivia, things would be ugly, so he was protecting her. Assumption was all I had, because courage was lacking, and I was not about to just ask her if he had told Alivia, and frankly Rachel seemed to be having a great time and maybe for just a few days had not been tortured by the turmoil they had been in. I then text Jack. His response was light hearted and somewhat silly for him. He said, "Thank you, Jesus, she's back!!!!!!!!!!!!" This response, of course, triggered another assumption: he must have told her. He was feeling relief, and that relief was allowing him the freedom to tell a joke, be funny, and not be weighed down by the misery he had been carrying. The next eight hours in that truck were long, quiet, and full of anticipation. When we finally hit Oklahoma, familiarity started to sneak in. I knew we were getting closer to home.

I was excited to see Jack, KK, and Pop, and of course the girls. Exhausted from a seven-day trip away from home, but refueled by the anticipation of hugging everyone's neck, kissing cheeks, and getting caught up on the progress of breaking free! We pulled into the driveway and hadn't even begun to unload our bags, when that diesel truck echoed down that old country road. It got louder by the second as Jack made his way up our driveway. He never would admit it, he worked diligently to keep up his hard exterior, but he was excited to see us as well. He had missed us, his people, his comfort, and his safe place. He stepped out of that old diesel pick up and made his way into the house. The moment I saw Jack's face, I could tell by the sadness and brokenness in his eyes that he had not told her yet. He wanted to, and planned to, but he just couldn't quite get there. He sat at the kitchen table, we tried to talk about the trip, but the destination of the conversation had already been determined. It would soon be headed to the topic we were all avoiding.

We headed over to KK's to eat dinner and celebrate being back together after the seven-day trip. As we sat and ate, Jack began to talk about the inevitable. He was ready now, he couldn't wait anymore, he just needed help gathering the words. We sat at the sacred table at KK's, looking at the beauty of those purple flowers, the colorful glow of the sun set, and we wrote down his thoughts. We began to take the truth as Jack Wayne was carrying it, seeing it, the hard painful truth of this very unfortunate detour and we began to try and put it into words.

Putting the truth into written word forces you to deal with the pain of the truth, but it also allows you to experience the power of healing that the truth carries with it. The truth from Jack's perspective was that Alivia had been a great mom, not only to Avery, but to his girls. She had been kind and fun, but their life together had been built on denial and the pain that Rachel had caused him. Even though it was built on those sandy shores, Jack did love Alivia, as a friend, as someone who had been with him as he had tried to heal from the heartache that Rachel had caused him. When you walk through fire with someone, it changes the dynamic of your relationship. Walking through fire is not something everyone will do with you, and it's not something you invite anyone to do. It is something though that deepens a bond, it's a game changer. I knew this first hand because that is what had created the bond that lived between all of us as well. We had walked this trail of fire with them, and we were forever branded from this experience. Although Alivia had walked with him through one of the darkest seasons of his life, there was still that harsh piece of reality that there was a very important piece of Jack that was missing that he could never give Alivia. She may be able to have him physically present with her, but his heart and his soul would always be missing because those two things had always belonged to Rachel.

I think one of the things that Jack failed to realize through all of this though was that now a piece of his heart and soul would always reside with Alivia, even if he made the decision to go back to Rachel. Alivia was the mother of his only son. She had walked that fire filled road with him, therefore they would forever be bonded in some ways. We worked on that letter for a little while that night, not too long. It was as if when we were done working on it, Jack already seemed better, lighter, and a little more free. We finished up dinner and table time that night, and he went home to Alivia. It was all so confusing to me. I had never walked one day in Jack's shoes, therefore it's hard to understand the journey someone is truly on, unless you yourself have walked the same road. Even when we walk the same road as our fellow man, we still have never traveled in their shoes. Our hearts can ache for someone, but to truly understand what they are feeling or carrying, it is quite impossible.

The next day, after the long night of letter writing, Rachel was heading home. It was late when she got back, I went to KK's to greet her. I had missed her so much. She looked even more kissed by the sun than she normally did, her blonde hair glowing, and her smile, well she wasn't wearing it. She wasn't crying or sad, just somber, much like the mood Jack had been carrying lately. She sat at the table at KK's, we looked at pictures and talked about our trips. The conversation of course headed to Jack, she acted as if she hadn't heard much from him. My heart was racing with anxiety. Had he decided that he was just going to stay? After we wrote down all the good things about Alivia, and the fact that none of this was her fault, had he decided that the weight of his guilt would keep him locked right where he was, or had he been reminded that she was his friend, and maybe that was enough? I tried to text him that night to check on him, there was no response. Baylee tried to text her dad, again, no response. As I left KK's that night, I left concerned. What if he had given her the letter and she had gotten so angry and something had happened to him. Every crazy, irrational possibility raced through my mind.

On my way home that night, I would be taking a detour

myself. As I approached the stop sign at the end of KK's road, I should have turned left to go home, but I turned right and I drove by Jack's house. That rustic farm house sat so far off the road, not one light except the dim light that lit up the porch that stretched the length of the house could be seen. I drove by once and tried to see any sign of life, or of his truck, but I couldn't get a glimpse of anything. I passed the house, turned around, and then went back again, still nothing. I debated driving to town to look for him, maybe he was out driving around himself. I finally made my way back home. I tried to lay down and go to sleep, but I kept texting Rachel, "Have you heard from Jack?" "Nope," she responded. "Have you?" she asked. "Nope," I responded back. I was trying to calm my mind, but I just couldn't. The next morning, finally a response to the desperate text messages I had sent this poor man. "Hey Sis, I'm OK. I'm not worth worrying that much about, but thanks for the prayers!" Of course my response was in full lecture format. "Jack Ray, you listen to me!!!" I continued on, telling him how important he was. Not only was he important to me, but to Jesus, too. This day in Jack's life, this trial, this attack that was tearing him apart and aging him by the minute with the weight of misery, it didn't catch God by surprise. God knew when he created Jack that this day would come. That he would have impatiently made a decision in his life to go on a detour, to take his life and his circumstances in his own hands, and that he would have made a mistake. The Lord knew that on this day Jack Wayne would stand broken, humbled, and beat down, and finally in a position of recognizing that he couldn't make it another day without God. He couldn't make it through this storm, through this moment, and he couldn't get back on his road home without God's help. Here he stood broken, sad, and carrying a burden that changed his posture, and ultimately would change his position. His arrogance and pride had created a posture that looked strong but on the inside he was dying. Now as he stood broken and surrendered to the Lord because he didn't have any answers for himself, although on the outside his posture was slouched and he seemed broken, he was stronger than before. He had become humbled, and through humility he had gained true strength, the kind that comes from the Lord, the kind that melts the heart of stone, the kind that changes our lives. Pride comes before a fall, and the pride that Jack and Rachel both carried in their marriage before their divorce was sure to create the fall that destroyed their family.

After my lecture I didn't hear back from Jack for a while. Later that afternoon, at random, my phone was hollering at me that I had a text message. Jack's name came across my screen, with a silly selfie he had taken a few weeks before. I opened the message, and a simple one-line statement opened up a whole can of worms, " I gave her the letter last night." I immediately replied, "What happened? Are you ok?" I expected a long wait, as the poor man is a slow typer. I thought, *"This will be a while for him to send me what has happened."* Much to my surprise, within just a minute his name came across the screen again, "Doesn't change how she feels. She's not leaving." I had read the letter that Jack had given Alivia, heck, I had helped write the letter. As a woman, I couldn't even imagine reading that letter and I sure couldn't imagine what I would have done, but then again maybe I could. Like I said, his love had changed my life. I guess I, too, would fight for it, no matter what that looked like. Jack was honest and vulnerable in that letter. He was as kind as he could be, but at the same time, he finally came out and just spoke the cold, harsh truth.

The next day that same selfie came across the phone as Jack's text messages started coming through. It was a declaration of love to Jack and a commitment that Alivia believed that God had put them together and that love bears it all, believes, hopes, and endures all things. The declaration of love finished up with this statement, "I will continue to pray for you, as I do always." It was like I was back in that gym so many months ago. As each piece of information of this tragic love story unfolded, my heart broke and I could see why this was such a hard thing for them to do. What do you say to that kind of declaration of love from someone? Someone that you have already told that your heart doesn't belong to them, someone you have told that the love you did have was built on pain and denial? What else do you say? Where do you go from here? How do you turn your back on that kind of grace? Jack's responses were short; I didn't know what his mind was thinking. I knew what his heart wanted, but sometimes if our hearts, our heads, and our words can't get on the same page, our heart stays imprisoned in a place of loneliness and darkness because our heads and our words can't gather the courage it takes to fight for what the heart wants.

I couldn't imagine how any of them felt, I felt as if I was riding on a roller coaster. One minute, I was sure any day Jack and Rachel would be free to be together, the next day I would get a copy of a love declaration like I got today and I didn't know what he would do, and honestly sometimes I wondered what he really wanted. This day, I felt like he was sure leaning on the side of staying right where he was for fear that he just couldn't bear the pain or the responsibility of hurting anyone else. Although when weighing that decision, thinking that staying meant less hurting, there stood those two beautiful girls, anticipating the reunion of their family, anticipating the day their mama would walk through the door of their home and they would be one again. How would he tell them that although his heart longed for that day just as much as they did, if not more, that his head and his words had won this battle and he and his heart would stay in his current situation, and maybe a part of his heart was battling for that, too? There was no right answer, he was at a crossroad and both roads led to pain, and he would be the one responsible for inflicting that pain, and that was something that was out of character for this man. That was a truth that was too painful for him to face, a burden too heavy for him to carry.

I tried to process the declaration of love as quickly as I could so that I could respond. I asked Jack that day if I could be honest with him. I giggled as I awaited his response. I am sure he was thinking that he didn't know me to not be honest. He just responded, "Yes." So I poured out my broken, but uncertain heart to him, "I think she is genuine, and that she is doing what you wished Rachel would have done for you, she is fighting. She is fighting for you and for your marriage and her family, and there can be no fault in that. I think you need to be sure about your decision, because I think she's probably truly seeking God out on this and you need to be doing the same. At the end of the day I'm not sure that being with Rachel or being with Alivia is going to bring you peace. Striving to bring glory and honor to God in all your decisions and how you wade through these consequences that is going to bring you peace." I continued on for several pages, there was no response from Jack.

I knew that Jack staying with Alivia was a possibility, and maybe that's what God wanted, I had no idea at this point. I also tried not to think too much on the reality that this decision would also be tearing apart another family. Avery would not know life with his mom and his dad. His reality would be not knowing his mom and dad together, but again, the alternative to that was him watching his dad living with his mom but his heart belonging to someone else.

Avery wouldn't be a baby forever, and anyone who comprehended love could see that Jack stood conflicted in his love for Rachel and Alivia, and someday this would be something Avery would see himself.

11

Fighting for the Dead

It had been a long week. Seven full days, one hundred sixty eight hours, since Alivia had sent her declaration of love via text message to Jack, and he then had sent it on to me. It had been seven days of awkward conversations, seven days of avoiding the real issue at hand, seven days of no one asking the one question that everyone was dying to ask. Seven longs days, one full week, one hundred sixty eight hours of uncertainty was pierced with that familiar sound my phone made when a text message was coming through.   It was mid-afternoon and I walked to the phone anticipating what awaited me on that screen. "Is God going to bring me a woman to put in my life before my marriage is over? I am talking about the first time. I'm just venting, had a letter in my truck when I got back from looking for a heifer. I should have been fighting for my family to the end is the way I see it, but the devil stepped in and won the battle." It took me a minute to put the pieces of this broken puzzle together to even know what Jack was talking about. Alivia had left a letter in his truck, I am assuming telling him she felt like God had brought them together. At this point, I had no words. I honestly didn't know the right answer. If I had the power or ability to find the "right" answer for Jack Wayne, I would have done that, but there was no way to find it, because in my heart, I believe the "right" answer didn't exist. Sometimes, well let's just say most of the time, life is not black and white. When the heart is involved you, can guarantee that there will be many moments of grey. Moments when your heart and your mind just can't get on the same page. There will be moments where your soul feels that God is telling you to do one thing and the world and your head are telling you to travel a totally different road. I wasn't sure where in the battle Jack stood at this point. I felt confident that his heart had already decided, but man, his mind was completely fogged up with feelings of guilt and pain. I took this moment to share with him my opinion, with the disclaimer that he should pour the entire contents of the next few text messages through a Jesus filter, because I was certain there would be a lot of Haley in there and maybe not so much Jesus. The closing statements of my time of testimony sounded a bit like this, "I know this is hard for you because you are such a nice guy and have such a very kind heart, but Brother, she's going to stay in this game, she is going to fight to the very bitter end to have you, your love, and her family, and if that is not what you want then you will have to draw the line in the sand. So if you have made up your mind, as you have implied to us that you have, then I guess go file."

Up until this point, I felt confident that Jack had made his decision, but there were moments when I wasn't even sure what the decision was. I think he loved them both. He loved them different, but he loved them both. He didn't want to be responsible for causing anyone pain, and he would be responsible for causing all of them pain. With all of this mess floating around in his heart and mind, I didn't know if he could give himself permission to follow his heart, and even if he could, where would his heart lead him? His next text clarified to me that he had waded through the doubt, if just for this moment and said, "I am going to file, but I am going to respect her request that I wait until Rebecca, her sister, has her baby and he should be here anytime now." With the death of Alivia's Dad being less than a month ago, she was trying to protect her mother from any more pain. Jack, being the kind hearted guy that he was, and because he did love her, was wanting to respect her request. It was acts like this that had me unsure of his confidence in the decision he was making. I responded to Jack's text and told him that he was a good man. I had told him that many times on this journey, and I would continue to tell him that. If you didn't have the great privilege of seeing Jack's heart, maybe you would disagree, but I could see the love that abided there, and the grief and heartache that poured out as he agonized over this decision. I was proud to know him and to call him Brother. That is what Jack had become to me. As we journeyed through his pain and waded through the disaster of his consequences together, we had become family. I had found a family that I had lost through my own parents' divorce. I had found the unconditional love of parents through KK and Pops, and I had found the love of a Brother through my relationship with Jack. I felt like I was gaining some ground on my own healing, but the cold-hard enemy, reality, reared its ugly head once again, knocking me out of the ring.

Jason had gotten a job offer that would relocate us about fifty miles north of Rush Springs. This was such a hard move for me emotionally. It was a great move for us financially and that was about it. I wanted my kids to stay in that small, familiar town. There was magic that lived there, people were different here, they would head home to raise families, to attend ball games, to be ever present with their people. This was rare in this day and time, and I longed to be there, to stay lost in the love of that small town. For once in my life, I had found somewhere I wanted to call home. Now, in the middle of this storm, it felt like we were abandoning Jack and Rachel. I was excited for Jason and his new job, and his new found adventure. I was excited to leave a mortgage behind for ranch housing, but the sadness and the sorrow of losing all that I had found outweighed the joys about ten to one.

I continued unpacking boxes at the new house, Rachel called and said that KK, Pop, Jack, the girls, and herself were going to go to the nearby city and get the girls away from that small town. As you can imagine, now that Jack had told Alivia he wanted a divorce, although she wasn't on social media posting her business, and the town paper had not printed the public declaration of their divorce, the entire town seemed to already know. The chatter of a small town is always loud, and normally was inaccurate, as far as the details that had unraveled yet another marriage for Jack. As the chatter got louder, Jack and Rachel feared their girls would be hurt by the conversations buzzing around the town, relentless like buzzards. They invited us to come along. As much as my heart wanted to, we opted to stay home because there was so much to do at the new house. I did ask if they would mind bringing up a few things that I had left at the old house. They agreed to do that on their drive up.

Jason and I were outside painting a few shelves to put into the girls' room, I was trying to be happy about the move, as I felt it was a great opportunity for Jason, but I was sure that my heart was crying so loud that he would sure be able to hear it through the fake smile I wore. We were putting the last coat of paint on the shelves and the familiar sound of that diesel pick up began to get louder and louder, they were coming up the driveway. For a brief moment my heart was so happy, the brokenness inside might have been glued back together for just a split second. Rachel drove up in her jeep, Jack followed behind in the pick-up. I wondered for a moment why they were in separate cars, but I knew. Jack had told Alivia that he was going back to Rachel, he had told her that he would respect her wishes not to publicly file for divorce until after the birth of her nephew, he had told her the cold, hard, painful truth. Even though he had spoken that truth to her, the other side of that truth was that he was still married to Alivia, she was still his wife, and he did not want to be driving around with Rachel.

Rachel got out of her jeep, as usual, that blonde ponytail coming out of the back of her hat. Summer had left its mark on her skin, and she came up smiling and reached out to hug me. Jack trailed behind her carrying in my microwave. I followed him into the house and thanked him for bringing it up. We exchanged the look that we had between us, it was an eye to eye contact, a simple raised eyebrow and a side smile that was a check to make sure he was ok. How he responded was always an indicator of how he was doing. A raised eyebrow and a smile was a decent day, a little shove and a big smile was a good day, and a raised eyebrow with no smile followed by a quick look away was a bad day. Today was a raised eyebrow and a shoulder shrug. It was new, but it wasn't hard to read. He was ok, but still struggling with what was right and what was wrong and the timing of it all. We walked back outside and he kept asking if we wanted to go with them. We reluctantly declined and they left the driveway, and my heart went right back to its painful state.

Jason and I stayed very busy the rest of the evening trying to get as much done as possible. It seemed as if the daylight just vanished and before I knew it the moon was taking its place in the sky. I sat on my knees in the floor of Lexi's room, the music playing on my phone, and her and I just hanging pictures and getting her room just the way she wanted it. I honestly had no idea what time it was, and the rhythm of the music and our work had really kept my mind off of the mess that they were in and the pain I was in to have left home. I bent down to pick up a box of nails and my phone began to ring. A picture of that long, black, curly hair came across the screen to let me know that Kathy Wayne was calling me. I answered in my normal upbeat voice, fully expecting her to be calling to convince Jason and I to go ahead and come over to the city and join them. My expectations were extremely wrong.

"Haley, it's KK," she said, almost in a short and panicked tone. "Hey, KK, what's up?" I normally would joke and try to be funny, but I sensed something was wrong. I could have never imagined what was about to spill out of that phone speaker through KK's voice. "Get on your Facebook and see if Alivia has defriended you!" I immediately obliged and then said, "OK, I am looking, but why, what's up?" I hesitantly questioned. Then KK's voice sounded sad, mad, scared, hurt, and any and all other emotions we experience, as she said, "Alivia showed up here, where we are, and she called Jack to come down to the lobby. She actually told all of us to come down, but he went alone. When he got down there, she punched him in the face. I wasn't down there and waited for a while before I went to check on him. When the elevator opened down at the lobby he was standing there, waiting to get back on the elevator with blood running down his face."

When this kind of information explodes through your world without a warning, without a prior announcement to help you prepare, your instinct is to just react. In that moment as my ears heard the information, my eyes began to imagine Jack standing there, blood streaming his face, and my heart began to break. I lost all sense and sign of Jesus, and did what any real sister would do: I freaked out. I wanted to drive to the city and find her, I wanted to knock her lights out, and I wanted to give her a piece of my mind. I was enraged. As soon as I got off the phone with KK, I called

Rachel. She, of course, was upset for her kids, and just about the whole situation, she seemed sad. I wasn't sad, I guess I didn't walk in that kind of grace. I was walking in loyalty and that is all I could think about.

After Rachel and I hung up the phone, I was getting dressed, telling Jason I was going to find Alivia. What I had found out while talking to Rachel was not only that she had punched him once, but several times, and he just stood there. Now I am not implying that he should have hit her back by any means. I just wish he wouldn't have just stood there and took it. It was almost like he felt like he deserved it. In reality, from Alivia's glasses, I am sure he did deserve it. Again, I was on the side of seeing his heart, not just his heartbreaking actions. I knew this was agonizing for him, and for her to react that way, well my mind was not allowing me to see anything but me driving to the city, finding her, and punching her right back. If he was not going to defend himself, I would do the job for him! Jason immediately said, "No, absolutely not. You are not getting involved in this deal, they will have to work it out." Not getting involved, well it was way too late for that approach! Not only was I already involved, I was in way over my head here. My heart was racing, inside my head it sounded like the pounding hooves at the race track. I was pacing, there was a sense of sickness that was floating around at the top of my stomach. As hard as I tried to keep my mind off of it, it was everywhere.

Rachel and I had been talking via text, I told her I was praying for them. I was trying to pray, but sometimes in the midst of tragedy and heartache you can't even find the words to pray. This agonizing feeling circled around me for several hours and then two words came through in a text that I sure wasn't expecting. "I'm sorry!" Jack Wayne's name and his silly selfie popped up on the screen accompanied by these words. What in the world would he need to be apologizing to me for? Before I could even respond, he said, "I guess now I am the biggest dick on the planet!" Now, I was very lost. Even if he were to be acting as the biggest dick on the planet, why would he feel the need to apologize to me for that? As I started to text a reply, the following text coming through and began to shed light on his reasoning for an apology: "I am sorry if I have ruined your reputation." I still wasn't quite following him, what had he said or done that had ruined my reputation? Then he said, "I just felt like I needed to say I was sorry." What Jack Wayne hadn't learned about me in the past 180 days of our friendship was that I didn't care about my reputation. My reputation is what people say or think about me, my character was who I was. I knew exactly who I was. I knew that God had allowed our paths to cross at just the right time. Jason and I would walk through this incredibly hot fire with this man who had gotten into a mess in life and would now be facing the cold, hard consequences. I knew that walking with him through this fire meant that I would be leaving the situation with ash on me, that I would be associated with the mess of their life just by being willing to love them through it. I knew that loving him through it meant that Alivia would hate me, defriend me, and make assumptions about my role in this reunion that were not true. I am sure she was assuming I didn't like her. She probably thought that I was sold out on Rachel and Jack getting back together. What she didn't know is I empathized with her pain. I didn't find a bit of fault in her and I wasn't sure who he should be with, because I believed his heart was torn and he loved them both but in different ways.

Throughout this journey I never once told Jack or Rachel what to do. Even if I had, I am certain that it wouldn't have made a difference. Jack and Rachel were wrestling with their own hearts, minds, and emotions. They were grownups and they would make their own decisions. It wouldn't have mattered what I told them, and frankly that wasn't my job. My job was just to love them. That night in those conversations between Jack and me, what I had already felt in my heart was confirmed. There are people that God puts in your life for a season, and there are people that God puts in your life for a lifetime; your people, your family, maybe not family by blood but whatever you have is sure thicker than water. People who love you, and people you love without any understanding of how you got here. How in 180 short days can you feel as if you have known these people your whole life? A place of familiarity, people you actually do life with, people who complete you, who are a part of your own healing, and you a part of theirs. There was power and life change when you were with them. Carrying the ash of the mess they made around was a small price to pay to find a family, unconditional love, and true healing.

It had just been a few days since the bloody incident in the city. Jack came home to an empty house. All the pictures of the kids and what was once their family were gone. Avery's baby bed had been disassembled, much like Jack's life had been, and his room left empty. That empty room was a visual picture of Jack's heart and just the beginning of the long road ahead. Alivia's things were gone from the house. She and Avery had not been staying there, and although this is what Jack had thought he wanted, it was still painful and hard. Alivia's black car came up that driveway, as it had so many days before when she called that place home. She had made her way back down that road of pain and familiarity to apologize to Jack and to the girls for her behavior. When I heard the news of the apology, I was overcome with shame for my own reaction. I reacted out of loyalty and love for Jack, but I failed to think about this entire situation from her perspective.

Alivia had experienced life, death, and separation all in a twelve month period. In just 365 days she had experienced the most amazing gift of life, by becoming a mother, 3 short months later, after she brought her son into the world, Jack would tell her that he still loved Rachel, and then just about 60 days later, her Dad would pass away. What does someone do with that kind of information? How does your heart even keep beating through the pain and emotion of all of those things? Grace had to be given to this woman for her "Rocky" moment. I wrestled with forgiving her, although Jack had already done so. The minute that she walked through the door seeking forgiveness, he had given it to her. His consistency to be a good man was not rocked by that moment of rage, he was like a steady old oak. I was like the waves in the ocean, as the wind of the circumstances changed I was swayed back and forth, moment-by-moment. That is how my life had been up to this point; inconsistent, back and forth, very circumstantial. What Jack was teaching me through his own journey of pain was that being consistent was powerful and it allowed people to see, feel, and truly experience grace, and that grace paved the road to the healing of the heart. Although Jack's actions were the reason that Alivia was experiencing so much pain, his consistency to be the man he was would also end up being the bricks that would pave her road to healing.

It was a very puzzling thing to watch unfold, I couldn't imagine wearing her heart around, lacing her shoes up and walking her road. If, for just a moment, I even let my heart go there, my mind was smart enough to know not to stay long, because what I knew is that I couldn't do it. I couldn't have made it one day in her shoes. I couldn't have loaded my sweet baby boy up inside my car, packed his things from the home I shared with this man, and drove away from that steady old oak kind of love; that strong, silent, and consistent love. I felt like every day I fought to keep my friendship with Jack not only alive, but healthy and growing. Now that I had experienced the kind of love he gave, I knew I didn't want to live one day without it.

12

The Breakfast Club

The summer days were long, but the nights were even longer. We were working hard to find a normal. Alivia had been moved out a few weeks now, and Jack had family coming in from all over. Jack called us and wanted us to join them. It was good for me and my soul. I was feeling like part of a family, I was missing home, and being back at KK and Pops was like ointment on an open wound, a sense of relief and comfortability. We pulled up to KK and Pop's house, cars lined the yard, family members were everywhere. This might have been the first time in a long while that I had seen Jack wear a smile. I knew the pain was still underneath there, but he was trying, he was putting one foot in front of the other and wading through these consequences with as much grace as could be expected, well and maybe a little more. We were all sitting in lawn chairs, sitting in a very jagged circle, conversations everywhere, then I heard a loud, happy, voice coming our way. I saw a big smile across Jack's face and he stood up to give a "man hug" to someone I had never seen before. Those watching this go down would have never guessed I didn't know this man. Jack introduced us, "Sis, this is my best friend, Danny." With no hesitation, Danny reached right past Jack and hugged me, and said, "Hey girl, it's nice to meet you!" Jason reached out his hand to meet Danny, no hugging would be happening with Jason. Jason was an amazing friend, and an incredibly sweet guy, but he was very guarded when he met people. If he loved you, he was all in, so he was reserved in his commitment, if he was going to love you or not. The night passed us by and with each passing hour, we fell in love with Danny, too.

Danny had been in Jack's corner, his soundboard. He had accompanied Jack on this journey alone, that was until my text came wrecking through his world. Danny was great comfort to Jack, he was great comfort to anyone. He brought laughter and light to every room he stepped into. It didn't matter if he knew you for fifteen years or fifteen minutes, he could make you feel like you were the only person in the room and that he had known you his entire life. As the hours passed, I could see that Danny was silently suffering behind his strength and his humor. He used humor to protect you from seeing his pain, and it kept you at arm's length.

Keeping you that far kept you out of his heart and kept him from getting vulnerable, and ultimately getting hurt. Danny was in pain, too. I wasn't sure what his pain was from, but he was also among the walking wounded. When you are a person that people depend on for strength, they depend on you to be the constant light in a room. It makes being in pain even lonelier. Danny had a few beers that night, and as the beer cans piled up in the trash, the walls begin to come down. What I learned that night was that Danny had walked through his own divorce. He was currently entangled in his own painful relationship that was full of drama, and although he hid it well, he couldn't carry Jack through this storm. Danny was in desperate need of finding someone who could carry him.

Healing is such a weird process. I had never felt like I had a home. My parents got divorced when I was nine years old, and after that day, my home was truly broken. I didn't have a place, or a group of people that were mine. I shared Jason's family, and I shared his town, where we graduated from, but it wasn't mine. It was his, he shared it with me, but it wasn't the same. What was crazy is that it had been 24 years since my parents had gotten divorced. I sure thought all the healing that was coming my way from that mess had already happened. I didn't even realize there were things I needed to heal from until I found what I didn't even know that I had lost; home isn't a place, home is a group of people. Wherever those people are, that is your home. For most people, that is your family. I had my own family now, Jason, me, and the girls, but I was responsible for creating a sense of family for my girls. Who was creating that sense of family for me? These people were now doing that for me, these people had embraced me, these people had become my family. This place had become my home. I begin to allow myself to be vulnerable and realize that I myself had a lot of healing to do. Healing was like laundry, it was a never ending process. It could be managed, but there was no final destination, healing was an ongoing process. When we left the family reunion that night, I was sad to leave. I was not only sad to leave the company, but I was sad to make that drive back north, past our old street, leaving our people back at home. With the sadness that encompassed our move, we worked so hard that summer to see each other as often as possible. With every sunset, every campfire we lit, and every meal we shared, the bond between all of us continued to grow stronger.

The summer days passed us by quickly and we would be sending summer on its way like we did every year in that small town. Every August, our quaint, little town turned into a tourist attraction during our annual Watermelon Festival. Our normal population was about 2,000 people, but on that day, there was approximately 20,000 people that would come through that town. The weekend was full of festivities and we would sure be spending the weekend back home with our friends. Friday night, Jason and I and the girls headed to the rodeo. Jack and Rachel decided they would wait for us at the house.   The news of Jack's new relationship status was buzzing around town, and Jack wasn't ready to face all of that yet.   He was also unsure if Alivia would be attending the rodeo, since she was in charge of helping with advertisement. We told them we would meet back up with them at their house.

As we approached the gate to enter the rodeo grounds, I begin digging in my purse for the cash to get us in. I heard Jason whisper slightly under his breath, "Uh oh." I looked up and saw Alivia heading to the window to take our money. I smiled big as she approached the window, I guess that was my way of waving the white flag, trying to make it less awkward, but that didn't help. She was very short and not pleased to see us. She was not pleasant and made it clear where she stood on the idea of making things cordial that night. The night continued to be awkward as I saw her pass by. She obviously felt I had some kind of responsibility in what had unfolded over the past couple of months because anytime I was anywhere near her that night, you could cut the tension with a knife. I was never so happy when we got in the truck and headed back to Jack's house. It was like I had been holding my breath all night when she would pass me by. Truth be told, I couldn't think about the situation much. I wanted to be mad at Alivia and not like her, but really there was no reason for that. As Jack had stated numerous times, she hadn't done anything wrong. I wanted her to have done something wrong, it would sure make this a lot easier.

Thankfully the truck ride from the rodeo grounds to Jack's drive wasn't far and my time in the truck to ponder the situation would be cut short. As we pulled in the drive, the flames from the bonfire lit up the sweet, country, night sky. Jack, Rachel, and Danny were waiting as we drove up. Danny, of course was in the midst of one of his crazy, emotional moments as a result of his dramatic relationship. What I now had gathered after the past few months of getting to know Danny is that he couldn't see all the good in himself, because he was too busy focusing on all the bad he felt he was responsible for in the death of his marriage. What he didn't realize is that he was willing to own his mistakes. He told me that he made a lot of mistakes in his first marriage; that he had cheated numerous times on his wife, that she had been his best friend, the one he felt most comfortable around, the one he could laugh with, and do life with. He didn't know why, at the time, that wasn't enough, but he knew his mistakes had been the reason his marriage fell apart. He was going to keep himself in the prison of those mistakes, I guess forever. He was now in a very unhealthy relationship. He knew it was unhealthy, being with this woman was almost like a punishment for himself. They were like fire and gasoline. It was constant turmoil. Every time we all got together he was alone, mad, and tortured. Bless the man, I wanted to shake some sense into him, but we weren't that kind of friends just yet. So we listened. It was also a good distraction for Jack, because he too was still trying to work some kinks out of his situation.

Everything wasn't as perfect as they had planned. For Rachel, dealing with the constant presence of Alivia in Jack's life wasn't near as easy as she had hoped it would be. Jack, dealing with two women in his life that loved him and longed to be loved by him, there was never an easy answer to that kind of dilemma. I hate to say it, but Danny, dealing with his crazy, almost brought a sense of comfort to all of us. Jack and Rachel didn't have to deal with the reality of their painful situation, I didn't have to focus on the fact that I had moved away from the only place I had ever felt like was home for me, and poor Jason, I am not sure it was any benefit to him. There were many nights around those fires I think he was looking at me thinking, this all started because you wanted to text that arrogant jerk and tell him we would be his friend.

Something else happened during those summer nights, as we sat around each fire, listened to every heartache, laughed so hard we cried, and became blood brothers and sisters. Yep, you heard me right, we let ourselves get lost in the world of careless kids and we cut our skin open until blood begin to flow from our wounds. We then rubbed our wounds together and we engaged in the physical act that symbolized the emotional journey we were on.

Well, actually Jack stabbed Danny in the leg, because he couldn't get the knife to cut his finger, but it was symbolic, really. Danny had always been the strong one for Jack and he didn't want to get vulnerable. Jack was forcing him to push some of his walls down. In hindsight, I believe it's because Jack was scared to be vulnerable alone. It was quite comical, but at the same time very significant of the love we felt for each other. When we cut each other and waited for the blood to begin to seep from our wounds, it was exactly what had been happening in our hearts each night. Every night another brick was removed from around our hearts, the wounds we had been dealing with in life that had been locking out the love that could heal us. That wall was slowly crumbling and without even realizing it, we were bleeding but we were also on our road to healing. You have to be willing to bleed if you want the chance to heal.

What I was realizing during this painful journey is that we were all looking for something. Rachel and Jack were trying to find their way back home to each other. They were traveling their road, hoping when they got there, they would find peace and healing. Danny was looking for love and companionship, he was looking for the ability to forgive himself for his past mistakes, and he was looking to find relief from the pain he was carrying. He was afraid to get real with himself, he was willing to settle for less than God's best, for fear of having to unpack that painful baggage and deal with it once and for all. I was looking for healing, a love that was unconditional, a sense of security and protection, and a family to call my own. Jason, well, I don't know that he was really looking for anything. He was kind of our constant in the midst of this chaos. He was just traveling this road because he loved me. There were many nights he would say, "Why are we friends with them again?" He, of course, would follow this question up with a giggle, but there were many nights I was sure he was not giggling on the inside.

The amazing thing is that we were all in totally different places, we were all heading different directions, but we were all on the same road, we were all looking for healing. When I began to think about it, I thought about the yellow brick road. Dorothy was trying to find her way home, the scarecrow, he was looking for a brain, the tin man he was looking for a heart, and the lion he was looking for courage. They all decided they would travel to find Oz, because they were told he could give them what they were looking for. When they got there, they were very disappointed to find out that the wizard was just a man, an ordinary man. What they didn't realize is that just by traveling the road together, they had found all they were looking for. As we all traveled through this tough time together, Jack and Rachel were finding their way home, Danny was realizing with each brick that he tore down, and forgave himself, that he didn't need to punish himself for his past, and I was realizing that all that insecurity I had felt all these years for feeling like I had to be perfect to be loved, that was a lie. I was far from perfect, and these people loved me just the way I was. As we traveled this road, what God was doing was using each one of us to bring healing to each other. He was allowing His love to flow through us, break through the stones we had wrapped around our hearts, and literally began putting the pieces of our lives together. Not back together, as some things once torn, never go "back" the same. Restoration is a process of making something better than it was before. The road we were traveling now was our road to restoration. This was all good news, but the journey was far from over, our road trip had just begun.

School had officially started, and it was harder to get together. I woke up every morning with a slight bit of insecurity talking in my ear, the devil taunting me, telling me today was going to be the day. Today will be the day you guys start drifting apart, today will be the day that you become a little less important to them, just like you did with your dad. Today will be the day they quit calling to check on you or slowly quit caring, just like your dad did. This was a battle that I faced every morning. Then one morning I woke up and Jason said, "Hey, we are moving home!" I couldn't believe it. I don't know why I couldn't believe it. When we had moved, our oldest daughter, Katie, who is normally very obedient, threw a big fit. She didn't want to leave our sweet small town, she didn't want to leave our friends who had become our family, she didn't want to leave any of it. She argued and argued, so I told her one afternoon, "You know what you just keep praying for what you want, and God will either change your heart or He will change your address." Secretly, I was praying with her, so when I got the news that God would be changing our address, I couldn't have been happier. We packed up our bags and headed home, and for once, in a long time, all was well with my soul!

This move back constituted a celebration. That first Friday morning we were home, we all met for breakfast: Danny, Jack, Rachel, Jason, and me. What began as a celebratory breakfast, turned into a healing tradition. With each Friday morning, another version of Breakfast Club was written. Each week it was a different story, a different kind of crazy, but it was our crazy and our stories, and we had each other.

13

Not Looking for a Fairytale

It was so good to be home. It was amazing to be able to eat breakfast every Friday with my people. The familiarity of that old highway brought great comfort and the scenery painted a picture of home in my heart. Life was good when I was looking at it from my view. With every sunrise, I would sit on my porch, no matter how cold. I would stare out at the sun, drink my coffee, and bend the Lord's ear. I would thank Him every day for bringing me back home, for putting the pieces of my broken life back together, and for loving me right where I was. Life was good for me, but every Wednesday as I passed Jack on the highway I was reminded that the struggle for Jack continued, and maybe it always would, maybe this was his new normal.

I was always heading north, Jack heading south. He was always driving that old farm truck with a big round bale in the back. That big round bale blocked Jack's ability to see in his rear view, this was almost symbolic of the life he was now living. As Jack focused out the windshield of his life, he was headed south, he was headed home. Rachel and the girls would be waiting for him, along with friends, his family, and the place Jack called home. With Avery sitting in the truck with him, it was as if for just a moment in time all was right in the world and Jack was whole again. In Jack's rearview, where he was coming from, was Alivia and all the pain of the past. The pain he was responsible for creating, but that good old hay bale was blocking his ability to really see anything in his rearview. The only bad news about this was that after he had his day with Avery, he would turn that old feed truck around and head back north to Alivia's. His windshield would be focused on Alivia and Avery, and the life that he left. The daunting fact that he would be missing out on so much with his son, the fact that he hurt a woman who did nothing wrong, but loved a man whose heart belonged to someone else. Those facts blared through his windshield like the hot summer sun, and he couldn't see in his rearview anymore. He couldn't see the remnants of home, the healing he had been feeling. That forty mile drive to take Avery home was always a painful reminder of the road he had traveled. It was a heart wrenching fact that he would never be whole again, that true healing and restoration may never be experienced for Jack Wayne. Man, that drive, it was daunting.

There were several nights that I would see him when he would have Avery, and as the clock ticked away and got closer for him to load Avery up and take him back to his mama, Jack would begin to get irritable, short, and a little more quiet than usual. I noticed this pattern in him after just a few times he had made the long, quiet, lonely drive to get Avery and take him back home. Every time he would pull back in the driveway, he stepped out of that feed truck alone and weighed down with pain, guilt, and sadness. Although none of those things he was feeling were anyone's fault, they were just consequences of a decision he had made, sometimes I felt like those of us around him that loved him were the recipients of the pain he felt. He would say or do things that were hurtful to those of us there for him. It wasn't who he was, it wasn't his character, it was just his reaction to pain. I continued to walk through the trenches with Jack, even though we never spoke of the pain he felt, or the burden that we shared, or the journey we walked, it was an unspoken journey we were making together. I was tired of hurting, I knew they had to be, and I wondered if the day would come when we would be past all the pain. Did that day exist, or was that just a hopeful, fairy tale expectation that we were never going to experience? Was happily ever after just for fairy tales? Could we fight hard enough in our own lives to see happily-ever-after? What exactly did happily-ever-after look like?

The winter was coming to an end on the calendar but in the hearts of Jack and Rachel, the winter was just beginning. With every fight, frustration, and harsh word, the temperature continued to drop, and hearts continued to get harder. The air was so cold it almost became painful to just be in their presence. They were trying hard to hide it, and acted as if nothing was wrong, but I could see it on him, he carried it in his demeanor, and always in his eyes.

We were still meeting on Fridays for breakfast, our group had gotten a little bigger and added a few faces, but the core group remained. We had met one morning early in the spring, it was early March, the weather outside was perfect. It wasn't too hot, and it wasn't too cold. I pulled into the small diner in town, and as I parked next to Jack's white feed truck, I couldn't help but smile. People dreamed of having friends like this. This was movie kind of friendships; man, I was thankful. I was thankful that in this busy life we all lived, that everyone chose to make this sacrifice on Fridays to delay work, or move plans around so we could have this time. It was just one of those great days. I walked across the parking lot with a little skip in my step. I reached the door, I took my sunglasses off and saw the crew all waiting for me. As I sat down with my warm fuzzy smile, I quickly realized there was some tension in the air. I tried to ignore it, but with a few sharp exchanges between Jack and Rachel, there was no ignoring it.

I made jokes and tried to be funny. Thankfully, Danny was there. He was always good at that. Just about the time I felt we had drowned out the tension, Jack's phone dinged to notify him he had a text message. He opened it, and as he did I could hear a little voice coming through the phone, "Ball," the little voice said. Jack broke out in a smile from ear to ear. As he smiled with pride, Rachel's arms folded across her chest and a look came over her face of pure frustration. I looked up and made quick eye contact with her, then tried my best to smooth it over. I reached my hand out, "Oh, let me see!" I said with a smile. As I watched little Avery look at a picture and repeat what it was he saw, "Ball," I smiled and then reached the phone toward Rachel, and said, "Here, you want to see him? He is so stinkin' cute!" With complete obligation and almost a bit of anger Rachel reached for the phone, looked at Jack with a raised eyebrow, unfolded her arms, watched the video and quickly handed it back to Jack. She quickly picked up her purse and said she had to get to work. We all said goodbye and as she walked out, Jack shook his head, but never said a word.

Danny, being the buffer, as I liked to call him, immediately began talking high school baseball with the boys, and we tried to pretend that moment never happened. I wasn't much engaged in the baseball conversation, my mind was still on the video and how happy, and how sad, Jack got in just a matter of a few minutes. We sat at the table just a little bit longer and Jason headed to the register to pay. Jack and I walked out the front door to wait on Jason. The door didn't even close all of the way behind us and Jack dropped his head and said, "I don't know how much longer I can do this." *"Oh boy,"* I was thinking in my mind. I knew they were fighting a lot and stuff, but Rachel liked to try to pretend all was good so I wouldn't have guessed he was here, at this place, already contemplating how long he could continue on this way. I filled my cheeks up with air and let out a big sigh. I looked up into his eyes. He was like a little boy, lost and sad and broken, and didn't know where to go from here. I raised my eyebrows and said, "What do you mean?" He looked away from me to answer. He dropped his head, and kicked a few small rocks that happened to be in the driveway underneath his shoe, and said, "It's tough at home. I can't do anything right. I am trying. I just don't know, we fight all the time. I can't say anything or do anything without her getting upset. I just don't know. I am going to try as long as I can and fight for this to work for my girls, but I just don't know how long I can keep going on this way." I have a real problem filtering my thoughts out before I allowed them to just come flying out of my mouth, so without thinking anything through I said, "Are you serious? This is what y'all wanted, you fought for this, you have gone through hell for this, and you're already talking like it's not going to work!?!? What in the world is going on?" He was still staring at those rocks he was rolling underneath his feet and he just shook his head. Jason came out, and Jack and I didn't speak of it again. I hugged him when we went to leave and as I put my arm around that skinny frame of his, I squeezed him as hard as I could. This was tough, this was harder than we all imagined. This wasn't at all what we had thought it would have felt like when they got what they thought they had wanted.

The last few months of school flew by and the same saga continued. The smiles on faces and pretending all was well, but the misery and burden that Jack carried, well once again, there was no hiding it. We were quickly approaching the year mark. With summer creeping up on us, we were almost there. It had almost been 365 days since they had made this decision to tear apart their lives in hopes of getting a love they had lost back. These past 365 days had proven that, "Happily-Ever-After," was definitely a battle - no, it was more than that- it was a raging war for Jack and Rachel.

It had almost been a year since Jack stood bloody in that parking lot. A year from the day Alivia finally faced her excruciating reality, a year from that day that Jack came home to those empty walls, an empty bed, and a broken heart. I could still remember that day so clearly, it was almost as if a part of Jack died that day, but at the same time, it was like he finally had permission to be alive. Jack and Rachel had fought and bled for their happily-ever-after, battle after battle, they had won a few, but they had lost many as well. It wasn't the place I thought we all would be a year from beginning to put the bricks of their lives back together again. Day by day, the mortar that had been shattered from the divorce would begin to hold the bricks back together again. This mortar was the residue of their detour. Alivia would now forever be a piece of their puzzle, she would be a permanent fixture in their lives. She now was a part of the mortar that squeezed in between the bricks of Jack and Rachel's life. Jack handled the situation as he did everything else in his life, he was steady to keep loving Alivia.   He was consistent in his kindness to her, and now a part of her would forever be a part of them. Jack continued to wear the weight of this pain and misery on his face, in the shortness of his temper, and in the distance of his demeanor. This wasn't as easy of a road as Rachel had imagined. She had expected it to be rough, but I don't think that anyone could have anticipated the pain, the heartache, and the turmoil that this battle would truly bring.

Although these past 365 days might not have been all that Jack and Rachel had expected, the rest of us pressed on. Not to leave them behind, but we were traveling our own roads. Danny had finally left his tortured relationship and he was picking up the pieces of his heart and his life. He was beginning to set himself free from the guilt and the pain he carried. Every day he was growing into a better version of himself. Breakfast Club was rocking on and our friendships were growing stronger despite the turmoil that Jack and Rachel were still walking through. Rachel continued to keep herself locked up. She continued to put on a smile and keep us all at arm's length, Jack was doing the opposite. He was bleeding out, reaching out, and wanted us to all be with him as much as possible.

I was discovering and accepting that healing was just part of life, and I was forever thankful that God had given me these amazing people to travel this road to restoration with. Something else very significant began to happen over that year, Jack and Danny begin to fall in love with Jesus. It sounds so cliché and I don't know how to really put it into words, but God is the glue. When you begin to seek Him and look for Him in the moments of your day, in the warmth of your friendships, and you let Him begin to truly take the wheel, you realize just how amazing it is to not be in the driver's seat of your life. You also learn to love yourself, not because of who you are but who you belong to. You begin to take better care of your family and your friends, because you realize those relationships are not only a gift from God, but they are your ability to see, feel, and touch a glimpse of who He truly is. You realize that through all the things that God does for you and the people that He gives you, He is molding you, making you into the best version of yourself that He created you to be. You realize that you were hoping to find a place of peace, happiness, and healing as a destination, but what He reveals to you is that it's an ongoing road trip.

Danny was healing because he was accepting this. Jack was trying to heal, because he wanted to accept this truth, but he was wrestling. Rachel was still imprisoned in the pain of her past, not just with Jack, but the past of her childhood and other scars she bore. It was hard for her to experience the same level of healing because she wasn't willing to be the same level of vulnerable. She wasn't just wrestling God with her inability to be vulnerable, she was wrestling us all as well. She was hiding her heart, in fear that she couldn't handle the pain of it breaking ever again. What she failed to realize is that when you guard your heart so fiercely, you leave no room to let love in. When the blood of love can't get in, the heart can't pump and it eventually quits beating and a heart that doesn't beat means a life that isn't lived. You can't live without love, it's just impossible.

The days passed and the tension continued. It felt as if we were taking steps backwards. We were back to the place we were before they decided to get back together. We were there in the uncertainty of each day, wondering what today would bring. Would today be the day they got better, or would today be the day their love finally died? My heart continued to ache for Jack and worry filled my soul. Every time I was with him, the misery he was in was like a billboard on the highway. The minute our eyes met, I could see the pain there, the uncertainty, and the longing for true healing love. Our expectations, many times, set us up for complete failure. Jack expected his heart to be full and right when he finally got Rachel back, unfortunately I think he was beginning to realize that the steady love he once had from Alivia was what he really needed. He was just too busy looking for something that he had once lost instead of realizing what he truly had.

Our expectation and desire for fairytale love stories sometimes clouds our ability to live and love in the present moment. Why we long for fairytale love stories has always puzzled me. Fairy tales are simple and really not full of love at all. They start with a glance, they end with a wedding, a kiss, and a carriage ride into the sunset. There is no real substance, no actual story, it's predictable, and that's why we like to watch them. Watching something and living something out are two different tasks. I love to relax and watch that predictable love story, but I don't want my love story to be predictable. I want the love story that I live to be full of adventure, passion, and pursuit. We must pursue those we love, we must be willing to do what it takes to attain passion, adventure, and friendship. We must be willing to crawl through the trenches with people, walk with them through the pain of their mistakes, in the heartache of failed dreams, and sometimes even in the face of death.

Truly, I don't believe we ever figure it out, but we travel many roads with many people that God uses to mold us, to build us, and to grow love in us. None of those things that create bonds and mold us are easy. Fairytales are easy, they are predictable and familiar and sometimes we like predictable in an unpredictable world. We like it for a moment, for just a split second, but we don't want our life to be defined by predictable surface relationships. We want the depth and the power of love, and with that comes the pain and heartache that it takes to weave our souls together, to be more than surface, to experience a love that leaves a story, a legacy, a life changing impression on this dark, cold, world. Real love is a risk, a risk that comes with a huge reward, a reward that is unattainable without it.

Jack had risked it all to have Rachel back. It was an answer to the prayers that he had prayed, the nights he had cried himself to sleep and pleaded with God to bring her home. He had gotten what he had wanted, and maybe he was forgetting just how badly he had wanted it, or maybe he was realizing that time had changed what he wanted.

Ownership of his heart belonged to Rachel, but protection of his heart was still the job of Alivia. Alivia was fervent in her prayers for him, and I didn't see that coming to an end anytime soon. Every piece of evidence of this love story, as it had did in the beginning, puzzled me even more. I didn't know how the man would every truly choose.

Rachel wanted so badly to make sense of things in her mind, but the harder she tried to understand, the farther out of touch she became with her heart. She was suffocating the love right out of her own story. Jack was so exhausted, wrestling with his own guilt and pain that he stood by allowing it to slowly quit breathing, knowing that as soon as their story ran out of oxygen, the heartbeat of it all would stop and for the first time in sixteen years, their love may truly die. Sometimes things just can't be explained. When it comes to love, I don't know that it can ever be explained. It's something, that hopefully, we experience. It's not something we do, or three little words we say, it's something we are a part of, something that molds us. It's the thing that we are most afraid of, but the thing we want the most. We pursue, we chase, and we work the majority of our life to find love, but many times when we get love, we quit doing all of those things. We quit pursuing, we quit working, and then just like that, the love we worked so hard to get, we have lost.

14

Worth the Fight

All of this confliction was flaring up and things were unsettled on the home front, when another bomb came wrecking through their world. Jack sent a text asking Jason and I to pray for Avery, he had been sick and would be having some tests done. Jack seemed concerned, he acted as if he wasn't, but he was as predictable as the twelve o'clock train. His moods were swinging like the pendulum on a clock. He was short and irritable, then he was remorseful. His remorse was never followed by an apology, just a light joke, and a small shove, trying to feel the water to see if you were upset, or if you were realizing his behavior had nothing to do with you. I was never upset, I knew what was going on. It was weird how I could read Jack. One night after an evening of hanging out, even Jason mentioned it. "It's neat what you guys have, your friendship is truly one of a kind" he said, with a sense of envy. It was, and I was very thankful for it, but at the same time it was hard and heavy to bear the weight and pain of someone else's life and not be able to do anything to truly help them.

It had been a few days since the tests were ran, Alivia had called Jack to let him know the results. There was a brief scare and a mention of low white blood count, leukemia might have been a word whispered, and all fear was inflicted in our hearts. Avery was sick and no one knew what was really going on, therefore there was no sure treatment options just yet. The waiting and the unknown was almost unbearable. During this uncertainty, the woman and the mother in me began to empathize with Alivia.

In a season of fear, rationality is sometimes thrown out the window, and we live in a place of vulnerability and reaction. The door that had stayed open for Avery to pass through between Jack and Alivia had always just stayed open. Jack was on one side of the door, Alivia on the other, but Jack didn't pass through on her side, and she didn't pass through to his. These boundaries slowly blurred with the news of their son. As the boundaries blurred, Jack allowed himself to get closer to Alivia through this season. Although he hid it well behind his arrogant persona, Jack was a man of great compassion. His heart was big, and he was kind, and compassionate, and soft. Not many of us had the great privilege to see the best version of Jack Wayne, but those of us who did, well, maybe, that's why we loved him so much. He didn't share much of his heart with many, so if he shared it with you, it was like you were among the select group, the real VIPs of Jack Wayne's life - we were the true insiders.

What Jack realized during this season of great pain and fear is that Alivia had him, and that was it. Her dad was gone, her mom was healing herself from the loss of her soulmate, and then there was Jack. Without even knowing it, and with no intention of doing it, he began to cross through the door closer to Alivia's side. With every doctor visit, hours in the ER, and every tear that Alivia shed, he couldn't stand across the hospital room another day. He would finally make those five big steps across the cold hospital floor as their child lay screaming on the table from another IV and more blood drawn, and he would embrace Alivia and begin to close the gap that once stood between them. As he stood in that hospital room and held her in his arms for the first time in over a year, I believe he may have found just as much comfort in the warmth of her body against his as she did, knowing she wasn't alone in this scary place we call the unknown. For once in a really long time, he felt a sense of companionship and reciprocated love.

During Avery's sickness, I began to reach out to Alivia a little bit, of course with Jack's permission. I felt a sense of obligation, I wanted to fill in the gap for Jack. I knew he couldn't be there to help her with Avery when he had been crying and clingy all day, so after Jack granted me permission, and with his blessing, I began to try to help her out. The first few weeks, I was very careful to keep my lines drawn. Rachel was my friend first, and my loyalty of course was always to Jack. I made these things clear my first few visits with Alivia. She was really good about it, she didn't mention Jack much, and never pried me for any information. I felt good about my decision to help Jack and stand in the gap for him, and to be honest I, myself, was finding a good friend in Alivia. She and I had a lot of things in common. We loved junking and crafting, a good can of spray paint and an old piece of furniture sounded like a night of fun to us. We loved good movie nights, Starbucks coffee, and trips to Hobby Lobby for our next craft idea. We were very different in some regards but we were very alike in many as well. She appreciated great music and was trying to teach me to do the same, I couldn't remember who sang what song to save my life. I was doing good to remember words, much less the artist, or what album what song was on. She was extremely organized and a little OCD, I was a complete free spirit, and needed a little organizing help in my chaotic life. She was a phenomenal cook, a cooked meal for me was a hot dog heated up in the microwave and a can of chili I cooked in a pan on the stove. What was fun though was that she was a good teacher, and she was patient. We started having food prepping days on Sundays after church, probably one of my favorite days, and at least one other day of the week we were together for errands and coffee. She was easy to talk to, she was a great listener, and she just made me better.

Summer was rocking along, the sun was blazing outside, but it remained winter for Jack and Rachel. We had contemplated a lake trip for Fourth of July, like we had done the year before, but at the last minute decided we would stay at home. We planned a big celebration at Jack and Rachel's house. It was the perfect summer night. Kids laughing, the smell of the grill, a blanket of stars over us, and the most beautiful fireworks. Jack's lawn was covered with lawn chairs, family and friends. Jason had put the tailgate down on his truck. Danny, Shay, his new, amazing girlfriend who didn't seem to be a death sentence for him, myself, and Jason all sat on the back of the truck swinging our legs like kids, gazing up at the fireworks. Rachel was in the house getting a few things, and then made her way outside. It was probably one of the calmest and most peaceful nights we had experienced all together in a really long time. Rachel was still wrestling with the fact that Alivia and I were friends. She had voiced to me that she wished she could just keep me to herself, but she understood. She did act funny though, and began to make little comments like, "I'm sure Jack is happy you're friends with Alivia now, I'm sure he wants it that way," in a very threatened tone. I assured her that Jack had made it no secret that he felt it be best if we all get along for the sake of the girls and especially for Avery's sake, as we would all inevitably be a part of each other's lives for the rest of ours. The rest of your life is a very long time to live in bitterness and anger. Despite Rachel's hints of frustration over her and Jack's current situation, it was still a good night. I remember when Jason and I left that night, leaving with a smile and thinking maybe, just maybe, they were headed to their road of healing.

It had now been a couple of months of me seeing Alivia a couple of times a week. Avery had been battling sickness the last couple of weeks, one after another, and Alivia had been confined to the house. Some days I would just check if she needed anything and try to give her a little company. One day, I began to notice something that caught my attention. During normal conversation Alivia would mention Jack's name a few times more and more. At first I dismissed it, "*I think I'm being oversensitive to it because he and I are so close*," this was my self-talk these few weeks. Shortly after I had convinced myself this was all in my head, Alivia came by my work to drop some stuff off. She chatted for a few minutes and then headed out. As her tail lights were fading in the window a friend of mine that works with me said, "Man, I bet she said Jack's name at least fifteen times in seven minutes!" Oh no!! Now I couldn't ignore it or dismiss it as something that wasn't happening. My heart began to ache and my mind race. I started thinking to myself, "He's talking to her too much!" That night, as I pulled into the driveway, I couldn't even think straight. Jason was in the garden just plowing away, I parked the car and met him there. As soon as he looked up, our eyes met, and he said, "What is it?" Wow, it was that obvious? "You look so far away, what's going on?" he questioned. I began to tell him about the mention of Jack's name that day at work. He immediately said, "You have to talk to him!" I leaned my head back, filled my cheeks to full capacity with air, and then blew it all out until my cheeks were completely flat again. "Why do I always have to talk to him? If I were him I wouldn't want to be my friend!!" I declared, slowly enunciating every syllable. He said, "Well, you are his friend, you're the one that knows the information. He is playing with fire and doesn't even realize it, and you are going to have to be the one to talk to him." He stated it very matter-of-fact, didn't even give me a chance to respond, and went right back to plowing his garden. I really wanted to pass the job off to Danny, but then again, I didn't even want to mention it to him. I didn't want to mention it to anyone, I wanted to pretend like it wasn't happening. I continued to wrestle with this in my heart and mind, but left it all locked away there.

The wrestling matched continued as I tried to get in bed that night. I began to see that he was on dangerous territory, and how horrible I would feel if something went wrong and I hadn't said anything. I really liked Alivia, and I felt like maybe he was giving her a false sense of hope. He had made his decision, he was with

Rachel, and he needed to make sure that was clear to Alivia. I thought it was great that he wanted everyone to get along. I thought it was equally amazing that he wanted to be kind, and still have a friendship with Alivia, but he obviously needed to make it clear with his conversations that he had chosen Rachel.

I still hadn't decided how or when I would talk to him, I kept praying that God would just make it all better, or send Jesus back, that would work, too. I finally told Jason, "I'm not getting in his business!" Jason responded with a belly laugh, head back, and said, "Well girl, it's a lot too late for that!" He did have a point, but I was trying to step back. That night we took Katie to softball practice, KK was there to pick Baylee up. I begin to spill on her what I sensed was happening. Immediately she slapped my leg as we sat squatted on the ground and in a panicked voice she said, "You have to talk to him!" "Oh my goodness! You're the mom, you talk to him!!" I answered her, raising my voice a bit, and again enunciating every syllable. I was beginning to think I truly was Jack's sister, we had to have been separated at birth. Without me even trying, or maybe even consciously aware, I was beginning to talk to people like they were the dumbest people on the planet. This was obviously something I had picked up from him.

She shook her head and said, "No, you're the one who she has mentioned his name to, you're the one that is going to have to talk to him!" Another head roll, with a huge sigh!! So I went home and wrestled all night with the words I would say. I just wanted to protect him, he was so naive to the ways of women! He was who he was, what you see is what you get!! He didn't understand that when he asked her about her garden, shared events going on in his brother's life, and talked to her about anything other than their son, that those conversations were fanning her flame of hope that he would come home to her one day. He was just being nice, trying to be friends. God bless this sweet man who didn't even realize what was happening right before his eyes. I drug my feet for a few more days, still holding out for Jesus to come back. I had finally decided that when the weekend was over I would figure out a time and a place to meet him to talk about it.

Friday had rolled around, I had a few more days before I had to have yet another awkward conversation with this man. Jason and I had decided to work on some flowerbeds, trying to keep my mind busy. We were outside when KK's car came racing up our driveway. Before she could even get out, she had the window down, hollering, "I'm so sorry Haley." She is always being funny, so at first I thought she was playing some kind of joke on me, but as she stepped out of the car I could see the tears streaming her face. Buck was with her, he slowly got out of the car, and began walking our way. Him being with her threw my thought process for a short loop, but then my thoughts went back to earlier in the week.   I honestly think it probably only took her about three seconds to begin to talk, but in those three seconds I rationalized every possible tragedy: 1) She had told Jack before I got the chance to tell him, now he was mad at me for telling her. 2) She had told Rachel and now Rachel was pissed at Jack and Jack had no idea why, because he doesn't even know that we know he's been chatting it up with Alivia. Those were probably the only two complete options I got out of my brain before she pulled out her phone, "I sent a text to the wrong person." She managed to get out through sobs and tears, and a bit of shortness of breath. I might have sighed with a sense of relief and might have slightly chuckled and said, "That's it?" She tilted her head sideways and with slight devastation in her voice she said, "Seriously, what do you mean, that's it?" She raised her voice a few decibels, as if I didn't hear her clearly the first time, and as if she didn't already talk loud enough, Lord help me, and said, "I sent a text to Alivia, one that I meant to send to you!" I'm pretty sure my neighbor four acres away could hear her at this point. Still with complete calmness, I tilted my head back to her, shrugged my shoulders and questioned, "Ok?" She turned her phone around so I could read the text she sent Alivia; "Be careful that Alivia isn't using you to get to Jack. I know you told her your loyalty is to Jack, but be careful. Maybe it's a good thing she is sharing so much with you, so you can talk to Jack about it." Alivia responded, "I don't think this was meant for me." That was the end of the conversation between them. I reassured KK that I was a big girl and I would go talk to her face-to-face first thing in the morning. What KK didn't know is that Alivia and I had been spending so much time together, so I knew Alivia and I could talk rationally about what had happened, and actually it gave me a window to talk to her about the fact that Jack seemed to be working hard to make it work with Rachel, although I wasn't sure how hard Rachel was working, but that was neither here nor there. What I wanted her to know is whatever hope she might have, well I felt like it was a false hope. All of this was running through my mind as KK was still talking, then the talking stopped. She seemed calm for a whole 1.8 seconds, but it was just the calm before the storm. She then grabbed my arm, gasped, and said, "Oh Haley! He has Avery right now! When he meets her to drop him off, she's going to say something, you have to talk to him now!"

This information did put me in a bit of a tail spin. I didn't want Jack to think I was talking about him behind his back, I wanted him to be confident and assured that my loyalty was to him, and it was, I just needed to get to him before Alivia did. My head began spinning of how I could meet up with him before he dropped Avery off. I didn't want to just show up at their house. I didn't want to talk to him in front of Rachel, for fear that she would think there was more there than there was, and I didn't want that to create a bigger mess for him with Rachel. I finally just text him, "Hey Brother, can I holler at you before you drop Avery off? You can swing by or I can meet you somewhere." He reluctantly agreed to meet me, he didn't understand why the urgency. I guilted him into it by telling him I had listened to plenty of his crisis and he could be there for me. He said he would text me. Not much time had passed and he said, "Just dropped Avery off, going to feed, meet you at Memaw's." My heart was racing as if I had just ran a marathon in record time. Oh my goodness, what part of "I need to talk to you before you drop Avery" was not clear for him? I begged Jason to go with me, to which his response was a light hearted chuckle, and he stated, "He's your brother!" Memaw's is only about four miles from my drive to hers, I think on a normal day it takes me about seven minutes to get there, but today was much different, it might have taken me four minutes to get there.

I pulled up to Memaw's driveway. I could see his lean stature in front of the sun as it was setting and he was out closing the gate. The closer I got to his truck, the sicker my stomach felt. I just knew at any minute I would lose my dinner. I parked my car and waited for him to pull through the gate. My heart was literally pounding so hard I felt I could hear it outside my chest. He pulled up in that old diesel farm truck, rolled down the window, and killed it. I hopped out and tried to figure out where to start. He acted a little funny, which I am sure to him I was acting funny. I had to do something quick, the awkwardness in the air was heavy and I was running out of time. I stepped closer to his window so I could fold my arms and lean on the crack where the window rested inside the door. There were a few more awkward seconds, then finally, I couldn't take it anymore and without one ounce of smoothness I just blurted it out, "I think you're talking to Alivia too much." Of course his immediate response was, "I don't know what you mean." Which in his defense, I really don't think he knew, or was doing it intentionally, but the reality was that it was happening and it was beginning to start a blaze in that girl's heart. As I tried to explain my perspective, I then had to tell him that KK sent the text to Alivia, and that was the sense of urgency for me to meet him. He was now the one doing the full cheek sigh, with his head back and maybe one small little cuss word in a whisper under his breath. I pleaded with him not to be mad at Mom that I would go in the morning and smooth things over with Alivia.

I tried to explain to him that these conversations, I assumed, were giving her hope, and they would be hurtful to Rachel. The minute that I mentioned Rachel's name his voice raised, his eyebrows did that thing they do when he got mad, and he leaned in a bit toward me, "Well hell, she's jealous of everyone. I can't even talk to YOU," he said with an over emphasis in his tone and his head leaning in even closer toward me. He continued, "She was pissed that I sat by you at the fourth of July party." I think he continued on for a few more seconds and said a few more things, but I didn't hear any of them. First of all, I was trying to think back to that night. The night I felt as if life was perfect. The night I sat by Jason, on the tailgate of that truck with Danny, Shay, and Jack, and we watched our kids run the yard, we smelled the burgers cooking on the grill, I barely remembered sitting by Jack. Then as he continued to talk, my heart shattered. I knew what this was. This was the beginning of the end of our amazing friendship. In the realization of that moment, my heart was shattered into a thousand pieces. Here I was meeting him at Memaw's to go to bat for Rachel and their relationship, and now I felt like she was sabotaging my relationship with one of the most important people in my life. I knew that the repercussions of a shattered heart for me would be a floodgate of tears. I didn't want him to see me in that state, so I wrapped it up just as quick as I could and started to get in the car.

His truck was parked right next to mine, our driver side windows side by side. His feed truck facing the road to leave Memaw's house, my car facing the field where he had been feeding the bulls. I got in the car, as soon as I felt the security of the door shut, there was no holding back the floodgates. The tears streamed my face, I leaned down to start the car, and put it in drive. I could feel him staring at me, my window was up, his was down. He glanced over and when I looked his way, my tear filled eyes met his. He started making a motion telling me to roll my window down. I politely shook my head no, made a circle around his farm truck, and headed out of Memaw's driveway.

I felt as someone had stuck a stick of dynamite in my chest and blew my heart to pieces. I wanted nothing more than for Jack and Rachel to be happy, and I had fought for that with them and for them for the past year, and even when I heard the news of her jealousy and the selfish act that would change the relationship between Jack and I, that was a moment I was fighting for her as well.

The drive home from Memaw's was much slower than the drive there. I was trying to dry up the tears. I must have had a flash back to Lamaze class, because I was practicing the breathing motions similar to when I was in labor. Maybe it was just my default breathing pattern when faced with an unbearable pain, but a pain worth going through for someone you love. I really didn't know, I didn't know much at this very moment, just that my heart was aching and I had no idea what the future of our friendship looked like at this point. It had probably only been about seven minutes since this attack occurred on my unsuspecting heart, but it felt like it had been hours. I pulled up into the driveway, Jason smiling, as he usually was as I pulled into the driveway. His strong, calloused hands leaning on the rake, and his cowboy hat shadowing his eyes, all I could see was his beard. I was giving myself a pep talk before I got out of the car, "Play it off, say it was fine, don't go into all the details, you will just start crying, and no one wants to see that, just say it was fine....." I continued this self-talk as I parked the car in the driveway and begin making my walk toward Jason in the garden. "So how did it go?" he asked with a little giddiness in his voice, just knowing he was right, and all went well, and Jack wasn't upset, and completely understood my concerns. I just looked up, forced a smile, and said "It was fine." Jason's smile immediately disappeared, he drug his rake behind him as he walked toward me, and with extreme concern, he leaned down a bit so I could see his eyes underneath that old, sweat ringed, grey cowboy hat, and he asked, "What happened?" "Nothing happened," I answered almost with a hint of insult that he would question me, "like I said, it was fine." He rocked his head back, walked around his rake a few times, and chuckled, "Girl, you have to know that I know you better than that." He just continued to look at me until enough quiet time had passed to make me feel awkward, "Rachel is pissed that I sat by Jack at Fourth of July." Jason's dark black eyebrows raised and his eyes got really big, like they do when he hears things he just can't believe, and with his hand that wasn't holding the rake, he pushed back his cowboy hat and leaned his face so close to mine and questioned, "You've got to be kidding me?" At this point my chin began to quiver as I thought about what this meant for Jack and me. At the first glimpse of my chin quiver, Jason dropped the rake and paced the garden.

I'm not sure if he was really talking to me, or talking to himself at this point, but his voice was raised and expressive, "You have to be kidding me right now. Can she not see that you guys have a one-of-a-kind relationship? That you guys are literally like brother and sister? Can she not see that you are good for him? I am going over there! I am going to tell her exactly what I think…" he was still going on but I cut him off, "You can't!" I hollered at him with a sense of panic. "Why can't I?" he asked with a head tilt. I took a deep breath trying to keep myself from crying even more, "Because when I left Memaw's he asked me not to tell her that he told me because she asked him not to tell me." Jason was a silent giant. He didn't go out looking for trouble, he wasn't arrogant or proud, but he was protective. "SO WHAT?" he hollered with his hands raised in the air, "I don't care what she wants, she is being ridiculous and I am going to tell her about it. You know what? He should tell her about it!! Did he see you crying when you left? I can't believe he isn't here! Why didn't he follow you?" I think he asked a few more questions, but I was numb, and I knew Jack, he would process what had happened between me and him at the barn, and when he was ready, he would come and talk to me.

Everything that happened with Jack Wayne, in all relationships, in business, and in life in general, they were on his terms. You didn't force Jack or push him to do anything, he did things his way, and on his time table. I knew we would talk about it, and I knew we would be ok. Ok just may look a little different in the days to come. Ok may be a glance across the gym and a simple wave, but inevitably, we would always be ok.

The more I thought about what had happened, as I was making dinner and lying awake in bed, the more sad, mad, hurt and somewhat confused I felt. I didn't feel all those things just for the potential loss of my relationship with Jack. I felt that way for what I heard in his voice about his current situation. I heard him say that he was friends with Alivia, he could talk to her, and he found comfort in that. He wanted to share what was going on in his life with her, and he wanted her to share what was going on in her life with him. All he was doing with Rachel at this point was fighting and putting out fires. There was no peace for him at home. My heart felt like it was bleeding outside of my chest, and now I had to try to still find the words to say to Alivia when the sun came up in the morning. I kept telling Jesus it would still be a great time for him to come back any minute now, but definitely before sunrise, that would be fantastic!

I'm going to say I didn't actually sleep that night, after what most would consider a nap. I was awakened to the sound of a text message. I rolled over to read, "Coffee ready?" It was Jack. I knew something was up, he never stopped by for coffee, and bless the man he could never just come out and say what he really needed or wanted. I assumed, this was his term, he was ready to talk about what happened yesterday in Memaw's driveway. Coffee was probably not on his agenda. Jason was still in bed, I hollered at him and told him Jack wanted to swing by. I responded and started a pot of coffee. The smell and sound of coffee was interrupted by that old diesel engine rolling up the driveway. I was prepared that day to let Jack Wayne go. I didn't know how he could keep his relationship with me and have a healthy relationship with Rachel. In the many hours I had laid awake that night, I had come to the conclusion that this relationship that we had was for a season. It had served me well, it had helped me heal, it had helped me believe in unconditional love, but I would be ok without him. I didn't want to let him go, but again, for Rachel, I was willing to do that. If I were honest, it wasn't really for her at all. At this point, I wasn't willing to do much for her, but for Jack, I would do anything. If letting him go would make his life easier with Rachel, well, then I was willing to do that for him. I had learned a long time ago to let my dad go for the women he loved, and I had learned to live without him. Learning to live without Jack should be easier, I was no stranger to this road. God had used Jack's love to bring a sense of healing to my life, to mend my soul, and now I was going to have to walk away from that. As I prepared to tell him to just drive out that driveway and not worry about me, my heart was in my stomach. It was hard for me to find words, which for those who knew me they knew this was very uncommon. I always had words, but today, my heart was unable to beat strong enough for me to find them.

He walked in the kitchen, for just a few minutes, he was nervously talking around and then he said he had to leave and get

Avery. As he turned to walk out the door, Jason looked at me, and pointed at him, signaling for me to follow him out. He knew Jack had come to get something off of his chest and he wasn't going to let him leave without doing just that. Jason and I had done some remodeling to the barn, so I asked him if he wanted to see what we had done. We walked out to the barn, and I showed him the remodel. He smiled, and said, "It looks good." I said, "Thanks," and we kept walking back toward his feed truck in the driveway. He stepped closer to his truck and I stepped toward the house, I waved, thanked him for coming by and turned my back on him.

I could see Jason in the window, frowning at me with disapproval, and still nodding his head toward Jack. I just kept walking toward the house, but my steps were interrupted by Jack's voice, "Hey!" I immediately turned, and if I was being completely honest, I was a bit relieved that we weren't just going to leave this hanging out here like this, undone, unfinished. I was thankful today his terms meant, we would talk about this, we would figure out how to say goodbye, and how to exist at a distance. He continued talking, as he walked to the front bumper of his truck and leaned back on the brush guard, "I don't want you to act weird around me. It wasn't about you, it was about me not giving her enough attention. It had nothing to do with you personally." I could understand that, but what was hard is I felt like he was the one acting weird around me. He was afraid to talk to me too much, sit too close, it stole the freedom from our friendship, it changed us. That was one of the things I had loved most about our friendship, the freedom we had to be us. He knew I loved him, I knew he loved me, we had a special bond, like Jason said, It was almost like a blood bond. We could tease, wrestle, hug, laugh and cry together, and neither one of us ever questioned intentions, or thought more of it than it was. We were brother and sister, no one could tell us otherwise.

I choked back the tears just as hard as I could, and I said, "Brother, listen, don't worry about me! You have enough women in your life that you are having to deal with. I am going to make this easier and eliminate one. Seriously, I'm a big girl, I will be fine." I knew the hell she had been putting him through. Her insecurities were coming out in a rage toward anyone and everyone, anything and everything. The consequences of crossing her, there frankly wasn't much worth facing those harsh words, the ice cold shoulder, and the looks that could kill if looks had physical power and not just the ability to emotionally destroy someone. He continued to try and plead with me, telling me that wasn't what it was about for Rachel, it was about him not me. But for me, it was about her. It was about her selfishness and her stealing MY relationship. I was very hurt, mad, and sad. The bad thing is, I couldn't talk to Rachel about it since he wasn't supposed to tell me. I would protect him at whatever cost, even if that meant this would be left undone, boiling in my blood, and making me crazy.   There was no way for me to be able to hash it out with her and get past it. I wasn't a faker. If there had been an offense or a wrong doing between us, we had to talk it out and get it right. If someone wasn't willing to do that, well then we were done. I couldn't be someone I wasn't.   It was just going to sit and brew and boil until someone exploded. He made his way to the door of his pick-up, yet keeping the conversation going.   I continued several times saying, "Really don't worry about it. I'm a big girl and I am going to be ok!" I was taking a few back pedal steps toward the door.   I was smiling, fighting back the tears, my chin was doing that uncontrollable quiver that sold me out every time I was trying not to cry. He opened the door to step into that old feed truck, he leaned his head around the door and with complete authority and a mind that wouldn't be changed, he said, "Well, I'm a big boy, and I'm going to talk to her, because our relationship," he pointed toward me and then back to himself, "me and you, it's worth it."   He jumped into that white, beat-up feed truck, the discussion was over his terms, his way, and just like that, God brought another piece of healing to my puzzle.

For years, when my Dad chose work, affairs, and anything and everything over me and my sister, what that said to me was, "You're not worth it!! You're not worth rocking the boat, you're not worth trudging through the mud for," and without me even knowing it I had been playing that tape over and over in my head throughout my life, and when he said those words, the ribbon was ripped out of the tape and God said, "You're worth it!" Through my tears and through the windshield I could see his big vulnerable smile. The one he wore rarely, only when he felt safe enough to let his arrogant guard down. I smiled back and contained my tears until I couldn't see his tail lights any more, then I stood in that gravel driveway and let the tears fall. I took in the scenery, I took a deep breath of the morning air, and I whispered a prayer of thanks for that brother of mine.

I walked into the house. Jason sat at that farm table, surrounded by windows, gazing out where that farm truck had been sitting. He didn't look up at me, he just smiled and then raised his coffee cup to his lips. He took a small sip of coffee and then, with a smirk on his face, he said, "Well, I can't believe it took him that long to get over here!" I looked at him with a lost look and an inquisitive smile and said, "What?" He just laughed and said, "I'm shocked he didn't follow you home last night from Memaw's." He sat his cup down, raised his eyebrows, plastered that smirk he wore on his face and said, "I told you it would all be ok!" Standing in the kitchen of that little farm house, I thanked God again for a big hearted husband who understood love, who was secure in his love for me and my love for him, and who knew that loving others made us better for each other. I hoped someday I would be as good at loving as he was.

15

He's Still Mine

Jack left the house that morning and headed north to get Avery. I would be shortly behind him to try to explain our text to Alivia, the one KK had sent by mistake. Jack had prepared the scene for me, so I called him and asked if she was going to be willing to talk to me, he said yes. "How was she? Mad?" I asked, almost afraid to hear the answer. "No, actually she was crying." He just left that there, no further explanation. I waited for a few seconds, thinking he would fill the silence with more information, but he didn't. "Why was she crying?" the silence finally forced me to ask. "She said she was just trying to be nice, and has no intention of using anyone, and doesn't want anyone to think that about her." I could hear in his voice sincerity, but most importantly I knew he believed her. He knew her better than I, although I felt like I knew her pretty well. She had impeccable character. She was a teacher, a lover of children, a kind soul. I didn't coin her as a user, it was never a thought in my mind. To be quite honest, the reality was, she didn't need me. Alivia Wayne did not need me to get to Jack. She held something much more valuable than me, and that was the hand, the heart, and the title of mother to his only son. Not only did Alivia not need to use me for that reason, it just wasn't who she was. She was better than that, she had character, she had integrity. I assured him I would take care of it on my end and not to worry. I also assured him that I believed her statement, which he quickly confirmed, "You should, because she's just a good person, actually she's a great person."

I texted Alivia to let her know I was on my way. At this point, I knew that he had been a little too chatty with her, but that was the extent of my knowledge, until that last comment he made on the phone. I began putting the pieces together, him being so defensive of her at Memaw's driveway when he and I initially talked, his chatting with her about just life in general, and now his proclamation of what a great person she was. I wondered if his regret was surfacing, if reality was knocking on his door and he was realizing that his expectations of complete healing and happily-ever-after with Rachel were probably not going to happen. I chalked all that nonsense thinking up to me being an over thinker, and pushed forward to get this very dreaded conversation behind me.

I drove up that gravel driveway to Alivia's sweet little house, she was out in the garden with her ear buds in. When I pulled up she removed her earbuds and gave me a small grin and a small shrug. I stepped out of my car and whispered under my breath, "Oh the things I do for this man." I shook my head at myself, my heart beating once again out of my chest, and honestly I started to get a bit emotional. I swallowed hard, talked myself right out of those tears, and walked toward her. "Hey, I just want you to know I wasn't discussing your life with KK. I was worried for you that Jack is giving you the wrong impression. It just seemed like, according to all your stories lately, that he might be chatting with you a little too much and giving you the wrong idea. I just don't want to see you get hurt, and I don't think he is doing it intentionally. I didn't know how to really tell him that without him getting offensive, you know how he is?" She smiled and nodded, but I didn't give her much time to respond, I kept talking, mostly out of nervousness I suppose. "So I discussed the situation with KK, to see if she thought it was that big of a deal, or just leave it alone. I didn't do it because I suspected you were using me, or because I was trying to talk to KK about you, I just didn't know how to handle it. I guess because I feel like Jack is conflicted. I'm not sure he is settled or confident in the decision he has made, and I'm just unsure how to help him, or if this is just a total assumption from left field and I have lost my mind." Before I could stumble through the last part, the minute I said that I felt he was conflicted, I saw tears begin to fall from her face. She nodded, and whispered, "Me too." The fact that tears were streaming her face, this alone was a big deal. This girl was a fighter, a suppresser of all painful feelings, a push through and get it done kind of girl. She wasn't the crying type, the pity party, feel sorry for me person, which explains how we had made it so many months without touching the subject of him and her and their mess this entire duration of our friendship, until now, until today, this moment. KK felt like sending that text to Alivia was a mistake, but I was feeling like now it was more of a divine appointment.

When I finally shut up and paused, she wiped her tears quickly and said, "Let's go in, it's burning up out here." She smiled and started walking toward the house. The smell of home cooked apple pie, or cookies, or something delicious greeted us as we walked in the door. Everything was so perfect, calm, and homey. Everything had a place, the walls were full of inspirational words, or beautiful pictures of her and Avery, smiling, happy, and living life. We made our way through the kitchen to the living room. On the way through she stopped in the kitchen, "Can I get you a drink?" She smiled and waited my response. "No, thanks," I responded. I don't know how she was doing it. How was she living, keeping her life tidy, and clean, and thinking to ask people if she could get them a drink? I couldn't think past their mess, I had no idea how she was functioning in the midst of it, and functioning quite well to tell the truth.

We made it to the couch, and honestly, almost awkwardly, sat next to each other there. She was no longer crying, although her face was still marked by the tears that had slipped out while we stood outside. She sat with a strong posture and she broke the awkward silence with a confident tone, "I love him very much. I know that's hard for people to understand after all he has put me through, but I love him. I have told him this, so I have no problem telling you also. I still have full legal, spiritual, and moral right to him. We are not divorced, and as long as I am his wife, I will continue to stay faithful to my duties as his wife. I will love him, pray for him, stand by him, and be faithful to him, until he decides he no longer wants me to have that job." I think she continued talking for a few more minutes, but I wasn't listening, I was lost inside my head. I had assumed they were already divorced. This put a whole new card in the game.

I had also assumed the past couple of months that Jack had been in a spiritual battle. I had even stopped by and told Rachel one day that she needed to be praying for him. When I passed him on the road, it was almost like I could feel the heaviness. I told her that something was going on with him spiritually. My plea to her, with tears in my eyes and complete, genuine concern was for this man's soul. That day I was met with complete resistance and a bit of an argumentative approach from Rachel. She wanted to tell me all he had done wrong and that he had yelled at her the previous day and asked her, "Well you try seeing your kid just eight days a month and see how good that works out for you." Sadly, I could see his point and couldn't see that she had a valid argument. I should probably carry around duct tape for moments like those, things just spill out of my mouth, I'm not a hider, "Well, he has a point. You have everything you wanted back. You have your family back, you have your house back, you have the cattle back, everything. He's the one who lost a kid, in a sense, and a friend." Jack had always made it clear that Alivia had done nothing wrong to deserve this, and that she was his friend. Rachel was upset that day, she said I was always taking his side. When we walked away from that conversation I was completely disappointed in her response, and I am sure she was equally disappointed in my unwillingness to tell her what she wanted to hear.

Knowing now, that Alivia had been praying every day for Jack to come home for the past year, made the day on the porch with Rachel make so much more sense. That day I passed Jack on that two lane back road, he waved, but there was such a sense of heaviness that came over me when I passed him. My heart immediately thought, he is in a spiritual battle, he needs help. That man wasn't in a spiritual battle that day, and every day for the past year, he was in a raging war. Not a war that could be seen, but an all-out spiritual blood bath. Today on the couch, Alivia said she had been faithfully praying for him to come home, and that she would stay by him and pray for him as his wife, until she was no longer his wife. Jack Wayne was in more trouble than I could have ever imagined.

I was wounded from Rachel, and I was vulnerable, I was also so sad for Alivia. I had been sad for her a year ago when her Dad died, and we sat with Jack at the cabin. Today, I might have been even sadder for her. I now wondered if Rachel had not already told the girls that day Alivia's dad had died, that her and Jack were getting back together, if we would not be standing here, and Jack would have never left Alivia. In the few minutes we talked and she was sharing with me some of the things she had told Jack, it was no wonder he felt in constant confliction. He didn't know which way was up. What I had gathered after he and I talked at Memaw's, and now after this conversation, is that he was miserable at home with Rachel. I think he loved the idea of them, he loved the idea of her coming back and him getting what, at one point, his heart had so longed for. He was now realizing that those things that made it so bad the first time around, which led them to the divorce, those things were still there. Rachel was still searching for her identity in Jack, in his cattle business, in any eyes that might look her way. She was still chasing her worth and her value in the expectations of success, and in the way Jack made her feel. This explained why he felt as if he couldn't do anything right, and he could never win, because he couldn't. Insecurity is a battle one must fight alone, no one can do it for you. This was his constant battle at home.

Here, at Alivia's, it was easy. When he showed up eight days a month, he could sit on the couch and wait for her to get Avery all ready to go. In those few minutes he could carry on a conversation, he could drink a cup of coffee, he had a friend, a companion and a reality he didn't want to face is, he still had a wife. Alivia was praying for him, she was fighting for him, despite all the pain he had caused her and continued to put her through, she would continue to fight, for their marriage, and for their family. I don't care who you are, when someone prays for you, there's a sacrifice that goes into that, therefore it leads to a bond. When someone is willing to fight for you after you have done them wrong, there is power in that kind of grace and forgiveness that you just can't turn away from. I was now the one crying sitting on the couch. I told her I was sorry, one because I was crying like a little baby and this wasn't even my life, two because I didn't have the answers for her. She seemed at peace and she seemed good. I hugged her that day, told her I was going to be praying for him that he would truly seek God and hear from Him and know exactly what it was he was supposed to do, because only God could clean up a mess like this.

Ice began to form on the friendship that used to exist between me and Rachel, the first sign of frost developed the day I drove out of Memaw's driveway. Rachel was headed out of town for the next week, and while she was gone, she suspected something with my short text messages. She finally asked Jack if he had told me about her temporary moment of insane jealousy. He, of course, told her the truth. Jack Wayne was a lot of things, but a liar wasn't one of them. The night after he told her that I knew of her moment of jealous rage, that diesel truck echoed through the trees as he pulled up in our driveway. It was a beautiful summer night, Jason and I were sitting outside around the campfire. Jack parked his truck, got out, and hollered across the yard, "Mind if I join y'all?' Knowing him, he wasn't asking, he was going to do as he wished, he was just warning us that he was coming on over to the fire. I smiled, and was glad to see him. Jason answered and said, "Go ahead," he knew the same thing I did, it was simply an announcement, really no need to give him permission. Jason smiled, shook his head at him and went in and got him a drink. "What are you up to?' I asked. That's all it took to unleash the war stories of his soul. "Oh you know, just living in hell," he answered, and then did what he normally would do when he wanted to tell you something, but he just wasn't sure how, he just left it there, in awkward silence, until someone would pick it up. Jason did the job, "What do you mean? It can't be that bad?" I knew how bad it could be.

I hadn't burdened Jason or Jack with the information from me and Alivia's conversation the day before. In all honesty though, I don't know if Jack even realized the kind of war he was in. He had a woman fighting a battle for him on a spiritual level, I'm not sure he could comprehend the severity of this war. I kept all that to myself, sometimes people just aren't quite ready to know those things. We listened and talked for the next six hours, until 4:30 that morning. I had thought that last year, when Jack was trying to tell Alivia that he wanted to go back to Rachel, my heart was hurting for him, well compared to this pain that was just a minor scratch. Jack finally decided he would go home, he couldn't stay in our backyard forever, reality was calling him.

He hesitantly stood up and reluctantly told us bye. As he stood up to leave I grabbed him and buried my face in his chest, and hugged him as hard as I could. The moment that I squeezed my hands around his back, I could feel his chest begin to shake. Tear drops dripped on the top of my head, my face shook from the shaking of his chest, and my face was now stained with tears. I wished I knew the answer for Jack Wayne, I wished I knew how to help him so he could quit walking around with his heart bleeding outside his chest. If there was something I could have done, I would have done it. As Jack and I stood embraced in the middle of the back yard, with the fire blazing, and the blanket of stars lighting up the night sky, Jason was walking around picking up trash. When Jack finally let go, and began to walk away, he looked at Jason and said, "Thank you, for letting us have this," he paused and looked over at me, and then continued, "brother/sister relationship." Jason nodded his head back toward Jack, then he said, "I'm thankful for you man. There are voids in Haley's life because of her non-existent relationship with her dad that I just can't fill, and God has used you to do that. There are things in her life He uses me to fill that you will never be able to fill. She needs us both. You have made her a better woman for me. I just wish Rachel could see that for you." Jack was still crying, he nodded his head at Jason, got in his truck, and left.

Rachel was still mad. She said she was mad at Jack, not me. She was mad at Jack because she had asked him not to tell me, and he did it anyway. The next six weeks as the words between her and I were few and far between, more and more words were spoken between Alivia and I. I was so hurt and my loyalty to Jack had never been more evident. Jack and Rachel were fighting every day, their world was in complete turmoil and chaos. Eight days a month when Jack would make his drive north and pick up Avery, his world continued to make sense there, and the more turmoil he lived in at home, the more peaceful he felt at Alivia's. Avery Jackson Wayne had the spirit of healing. He was bringing a bit of healing back to Jack's life. I don't know what happened during these last couple of months, in a sense it was almost like we literally lived through a full raging war and we couldn't see much due to the dust and fog from the smoke of firearms.

If there was any love left between Jack and Rachel, it was hard to see lately. They had been fighting every day for months, they were disconnected, hard hearted, and apparently suffered from amnesia, because they must have forgotten all that they had went through the past year previous. The months they sat at KK's table longing for their great reunion, working up the courage to tell their spouses that they wanted to be together. Jack had never said an ill word about Alivia, but all the ways she had shown love to him before he had asked her to move out, he had never seen as love before, because he was too distracted chasing something that no longer belonged to him. The night we stood in the yard until 4:30 in the morning, he went through all the ways Alivia had always shown her love for him. When he started the list, he almost sounded shocked, like he couldn't believe that he didn't see it before. "She always treated me like a king, hell, she still does. She gave me my space, she let me be me, and she never expected me to be someone I wasn't. Can you believe, that when we first started dating, I told her a part of me would always love Rachel, and she loved me anyway?" He asked this with no expectation of a response, and continued disgusted with himself, as he was having these revelations. In the midst of all this fighting, it was as if I could read his mind. If I literally could have, I think he would have been playing this monologue in his head, "What would life be like if I just went back? It was easy with her, not much fighting, not much expectation of me to be anything other than who I am, what would life look like getting back to that place?" He shared his frustration and his sense of confusion, sometimes without words, just with the misery on his face, or his short temper, or his silence, and his distance from those of us who loved him the most. This went on for weeks. I tried to figure it out, then one night I just watched him, again watching her. I didn't try to understand the mess, or the pain, I just tried to get lost in the gaze. The gaze that I once saw that silenced a gym, the gaze that revealed a love story so strong that I didn't even know their names, but I knew their hearts were connected, their souls were woven together and I saw a picture of love I had never seen from the outside looking in. It wasn't there, he wasn't watching her like he had watched her before. He was there with us, but his heart was somewhere else.

There had been so much anger, so much pain, and so many hurtful words exchanged between them the past several months, that the look had changed a bit. I couldn't see what his heart wanted, it was clouded by all the pain and the confusion. The mourning he was experiencing, as he was realizing that the friendship that he wanted to keep with Alivia wasn't going to be a possibility if he wanted to keep Rachel, he wore that sadness like a black coat at a funeral. Jack was a man that most would describe as a loner, he spoke to people and he attended events, he was out and about in the community, but he kept to himself. Until Jason and I came along, he was close with Danny, that's it. It was a bit surprising figuring out how much he cherished his friendships, since he was such a loner. I wondered if that was part of this harsh realization for him, once he got what he thought he wanted, it wasn't what he wanted at all. He wanted friendship, stability, someone he could count on and a build a life with. The old saying rings true many times, "You don't know what you have until it's gone." I believe, Jack was realizing he just might have had in Alivia, what he really wanted.

Here we were, what felt like another cross road in the life of Jack Wayne. He was being forced to lose his friendship with Alivia. I remembered an afternoon, we had sat on the dock at the cabin, Jack was very bold in his declaration to Rachel that he desired to keep Alivia's friendship. He told Rachel then, with no apologies, that Alivia hadn't done anything to hurt him, and she had done nothing wrong to deserve the pain that he would be causing her. I remembered very clearly asking Rachel that day, "Well, how do you think that is going to be for you? You know you and Jack were "just friends" when your paths began to cross again." Jack looked at Rachel in anticipation of her response after he gave me a small "Thank you," glance, for saying what he was having trouble just coming right out and asking. Without hesitation Rachel answered, "No, I want him to be her friend, I know they have a child together and they are going to have to work together for him."   Rachel, going back on her bold assurance that she wanted Alivia and Jack to remain friends, frankly seemed to be pushing him closer to Alivia. He obviously enjoyed his friendship with her, and what I was realizing is that loving Alivia made Jack better. Alivia was easy for Jack to love, she was there to love him, serve him, and although not the original owner of his heart, she was definitely the protector of it. If Jack chose Rachel and was forced to end his friendship with Alivia, I think he would always struggle with that loss. He would struggle with losing her spiritual strength in his life, and regretfully he would forever struggle not being able to call her friend.

Rachel, on the other hand, was in a tough place in her life. She was hard to love. She had literally built Alcatraz around her heart, and getting on the inside was a chore in and of itself. That night as I watched him watch her, I saw regret. Not just in his eyes, but in hers, too. I saw fear, sadness, and pain. I am sure, somewhere in there, Jack Wayne still loved Rachel, for obvious reasons; they had two beautiful daughters who were quite amazing, they had history, they had a past, the question was becoming, would they have a future?

I could relate to Rachel in one regard, I believe she had been hurt a lot in life. I'm not sure what all her struggles were, and I'm not certain that some of them weren't self-inflicted, but nonetheless, they were wounds, and they were struggles, and they caused pain. When we have been hurt, our default is to love guarded and behind walls. When we try to love hurt, we are still hurting, and hurting people continue to hurt other people. It's a vicious cycle, we can't seem to break free from, until someone decides to quit keeping score and decides that love is worth more than a win. Sometimes, people can't let go of the scoreboard. Their pride tells them that they have to finish on top, they have to win this fight, otherwise they are less valuable, and they need that win in their life to feel valued and of any worth. The truth is, love is worth not getting the win. If not winning means I have to remove the painful poison of pride and show you that I love you first so that you can love me back, then I'll take that loss. Love heals the soul and mends the broken heart, true unbridled love has that kind of power. When we limit love to live behind the walls of our past and our pain, we limit the healing power that lies within letting love in, and we deny those we love the piece of ourselves that we could give them if we would just let love out from behind those walls.

Danny was figuring it out, slowly but surely. He had finally begun to allow God's love to break down the walls of his life and he was able to love someone back. He found an amazing woman that God was using to teach him more about himself every day. Danny was still loving scared, but he was willing to work on breaking those walls down, it was an everyday process. He was not only working on breaking his own walls down, he was having to love steady and strong so that Shay would feel the confidence and the security to allow some of her walls to crumble. The battle was raging for them as well. If the enemy can keep us locked up in our pride, he can paralyze us from our progress.

Every day another brick was falling from around my heart as well. It had taken Jason many years to get in behind the walls that I had built to protect my heart. He had done an incredible job at loving me and helping me heal, but there was still a piece missing. When that steady oak kind of love came crashing into my life through Jack, I not only loved my family better, I embraced God's love more in a deeper way than I had ever done before. I am not going to lie, there were days where the fear of the risk would creep in, and my immediate reaction was to draw back. I was so fearful of losing people, and hurting again. When this fear would begin to whisper in my ear, I wanted to do my default thing and build a wall. God kept reminding me I couldn't do that, because we were on this journey together. My inability to allow God's love in to break down the walls in my life and begin to conform me, it didn't just affect me. It would affect the people in my path in life that needed to feel that love, who needed that healing, that I couldn't give to them because I wasn't willing to take the risk. So I pushed past the fear and the hurt and kept letting the love in, and I continued to heal.

Rachel, on the other hand, was hurting and unwilling to embrace any more pain, even if it meant she would be on her road to healing.   She was hurt from her own decisions, from her decision to break Jack's heart all those years ago. She was hurt from the pain of her past, her regret, and her own guilt. She was bleeding from those past wounds, and now she was dying from the new wounds that this journey had created. The fact that it had been a year now and Jack was still not divorced, that caused more pain and fear. This pain and fear and insecurity began seeping out in the words she said, the way she treated this man that she loved, and it was not only destroying her from the inside out, it was destroying them.

She was trying to right her wrong and come home to Jack, but sometimes it is just not that easy to right a wrong. Sometimes righting a wrong is accepting the painful consequences of our decisions, and moving forward, instead of trying to drive our car forward but staring in the rearview mirror. There was more pain to process than she had imagined, there were more walls than she was willing to climb, and there were still bags left to be unpacked from the first time they had walked away from each other. It was all too much. It was overwhelming. It was suffocating the love and the healing right out of their story.

16

Stuck In Neutral

Trouble continued at home for Jack. Rachel and I continued to tolerate each other because we both loved him. Jason continued to tell me that I couldn't choose sides if I chose Jack. I couldn't choose Alivia, although my friendship with her was amazing and genuine. My friendship with Rachel, at this point, was obligatory and painful. As usual, I knew Jason was right. If Jack stayed right where he was, with Rachel, which was a huge possibility, he had gone through a lot to be with her, then I couldn't choose Alivia, unless I was willing to lose Jack. Jason would run through this several times a week lately. I really think that every time we left the house, he would go through it again. Lord help the man, he knew me well. He would say it in almost a teacher to student tone, "OK, Haley, you can't choose sides if you choose Jack. You can like both Alivia and Rachel, but you can't choose sides, because we never know from day to day who the man is going to choose." When he would finish his lecture he would lean his head in a bit, as to ask me, "Got it?" I would roll my eyes and mutter under my breath as I would walk to the door.

It was finally fall, my favorite time of the year. Every year at the beginning of fall, which also happen to be Jack, KK, and I's birthday month, "The Month of Greatness" we had named it, we would travel to Kansas to a cattle sale. I was working hard at my relationship with Rachel, I wanted to do that for Jack. I had decided that I would start fresh, talk to her, and be honest. It was Wednesday night, the night before we would head to Kansas. We had some last minute things to grab, so we decided to run our errands together. The girls were all playing at KK's, and Rachel and I headed to town. We had a great talk in the truck, and I was able to be open and honest and get some things off my chest. I felt better about working at my relationship with Rachel and was starting to look forward to the weekend away. I had somewhat been dreading it since all the tension was very alive and lurking. Right about the time I started to feel like all was going well, we started to pull up in Jack's driveway, and Rachel said, "Yeah, it's just hard. You know Jack will talk to you about stuff he won't even talk to me about."

"Well, try not to bite his head off for everything he says and does, and accuse him of things he's not even doing, and that might help your lines of communication." That's what I wanted to say, but I refrained myself. I was trying to collect my thoughts and find a much nicer way to encourage her to work on their friendship when these asinine words busted through my thought process, "I mean, I know he loves you more than he loves me, even my mom has noticed it, even one of Jack's friends, and even KK." At this point my blood was boiling, for so many reasons, but I laughed and said, "Girl we aren't even in the same category! He's not into me, there is no attraction whatsoever in that regard. I can't believe you would even think that way." She tried to play it off as it all being her mom's idea. I knew the only friend of Jack's that Rachel spoke to was Danny. I knew Danny would never say anything like that. KK loved me like a daughter, invited me over for family reunions, holidays, birthday parties, and Saturday morning breakfast with the family. I sure think if she thought something was going on between Jack and I she would not be arranging such events with all of us. The effort for me to work on my relationship with her didn't last long.

I drove up in the driveway at home. The small security light was lighting up the barn, I could see Jason out feeding the horses. The lights in the kitchen were stretching out the sidewalk from all the windows, and I could see the girls in the kitchen at the table. I took the short walk to the barn in the crisp, fall air, and I walked up to Jason at first somewhat laughing, then the laugh turned to anger. "You know what, I am choosing sides, I don't care what you say, I'm doing it. I'm choosing Alivia, she's my friend, she's a good friend, and if Jack doesn't like that, well, then I guess I am willing to lose him." I got all of that out without taking one breath and with each word my voice level was raising louder and louder. Jason started smiling and kind of chuckled as he bent down to get the flakes of hay to carry out to the stalls. I crossed my arms and followed him, almost marching, as my folded arms bounced up and down with each step, "This isn't funny, I am serious." I had more to say, but he cut me off, "Yeah right, you ain't choosin' anyone over that boy." He turned to check my temperature before he continued, "I mean you better choose me over him," he did another quick glance back and smiled, " but we all know that when it comes to anyone else other than me, you're choosing him. Don't try to fool yourself." He chuckled again, then asked, "Where did that come from anyway?" In the most tattle tale voice I had probably spoken in since I was in junior high, I said, "Oh well, let me just tell you!" He threw the hay to the horses over the fence, turned to look at me with his big eyes that he always got when he was caught by surprise, and he said, "Oh boy, I have a feeling this is going to be good." As we walked back up to the barn I raged on like a lunatic about how ridiculous Rachel was and how asinine her thought process was. I also declared that I would be sick tomorrow because I would refuse to go and pretend like everything was just great while we were in Kansas for a whole weekend with them.   Jason was his normal, calm, steady self, "Hales, why do you listen to her? First of all, what you should have said, was, 'Yes I am a much better friend to him than you are. You are absolutely right!'" I laughed, he smiled that big smile he had, and said, "Seriously, we are going for Jack, he needs our help at this cattle sale, and that's what we are going to do. Honestly, if I were you, I would holler at him tomorrow and tell him what she said." "No, I'm not going to do that to him. I don't want him to feel like he has to choose and I know he already stresses enough before these sales, I will just keep it to myself," I said in a pouty little tone as I raised my head up and turned it away from him. "Well, that's up to you, but we are going, and we," he paused to raise his eyebrows and swing his hand back and forth between me and him, "are going to have fun!!" I took a deep breath and walked back up to the house with him. He was right, I would survive.

The weekend was long and awkward. I worked hard to not sit too close to Jack, or talk too much to him.   He just kept being his normal self. He was oblivious to the latest accusation, so he was still tackling me in the hotel lobby, standing outside the elevator not letting us go to our rooms, you know, typical brother stuff. I was a nervous wreck at first, then Jason, in his calm, assuring tone leaned over the first night and said, "Don't worry about her, she's miserable, that's not your fault. Be here with us, enjoy this time, have fun, let her be unhappy by herself." I wish it were that easy for me, but I immediately started beating myself up. Did I do something wrong? Is it my fault? I battled this all weekend. I was never so happy to see that "Small Town, Big Heart" sign in all my life, as we pulled into the magical place we called home.

Jack remained in the dark about the conversation accusing him of loving me more than her, and he remained in the dark about many other things as well. I'm not sure how he could be in the dark, the tension in the room was so thick I felt like not only could I have cut it with a knife, at times I was sure I could see it. We struggled along for the next few weeks. I avoided Jack as much as possible, because I knew with just the right glance, he would know something was going on. I would catch moments where I felt like he was glad the friendship between Rachel and I was ice cold, it reaffirmed what I am sure he already knew, that I was on his side. Whatever happened I would stand by Jack. It didn't mean that I didn't acknowledge his responsibility in the mess, I did, and I told him the truth about the things I felt and saw, but it did mean I would be loyal to him. I would stand by him no matter how the storm raged, or what kind of destruction it brought with it.

It had now been several weeks since the cattle sale in Kansas. Mine and Rachel's relationship continued to just exist and struggle through. I had built a huge wall around my own heart where she was concerned. It was just a couple of weeks before Thanksgiving, the holidays were quickly approaching us. I was still praying every day for Jack to make the right decision, to be the man I knew God had created him to be. I saw so much potential in the heart of that man, I just wanted him to see it, too. I wanted him to see that God had given him influence. Despite the fact that he had a quiet, loner personality, people were attracted to Jack Wayne. I don't know if it was the mystery of him, or that other people could also see that there was kindness and goodness behind his arrogant façade and they, too, wanted to see that side of him. I really don't know. I do know that God had a plan for him, and the enemy was working overtime to make sure that plan was detoured as much as possible until Jack Wayne would hit a dead end.

Rachel texted me and asked me if she could take me to get my nails done for my birthday. We were unable to do anything during my birthday week since we were in Kansas working the sale, and we had been busy catching up with the kids' activities and chores when we got home. This was the first chance we would have to get together. I was somewhat reluctant. Our relationship had been far from ideal lately, but I was thankful for the gesture, it was nice. I was hoping we would try to just be friends outside of Jack and their crisis. Really, when I thought about it, our friendship was built on and had revolved around Jack and Rachel's crisis. I don't know if Rachel and I had a friendship outside of that. I decided today would be the day I would try to make that happen. I vowed not to bring anything up about Jack or their situation, I would try to find other things to talk about. On the way to the salon to get our nails done, the plan worked.   On the way home, my plan was interrupted by one of the most odd questions I have ever been asked. Well maybe it's not the oddest question, it's just that coming from the person who asked it, made it very odd. Right about the time we hit the outskirts of our tiny town, Rachel, very matter of fact, asked me, "So, do you know what is going on with Jack and Alivia? Like are they going to get a divorce or what?" I'm certain my face was saying what the good Lord would not allow me to say with my words. It took me a second to compose my words, "I have no idea what you're talking about!" I took a deep breath and looked out the window.   She just continued talking, "Well, that makes sense. They aren't going to talk about it in front of you, now that you told them the first time they were talking too much. I just don't know what is going on or what he is doing." She said so many more things, but I had blocked her out, about like I had the last several months, every time she got on a bash Jack kick. I let her talk for the duration of the drive.

We pulled up to where my car was parked and I really wanted to just tell her thanks for the gift and get in my car, but again, the Lord doesn't always let me do what I want to do. So I looked her in the eye, took a deep breath, and prepared to speak the cold hard truth. "Listen Rachel, I don't know why you are waiting on them to tell you if they are getting a divorce or not. I don't know why you continue to live with a married man who has had a year to get a divorce, well it is November, so actually he has had a year and almost a half to get a divorce, and has not. Well, if we are being real honest, let me just say, I don't know why you moved in with him in the first place. I told you from the beginning that he needed some time and I wouldn't move in with him until y'all were married if I were you. So no, I am sorry I can't answer the original question you asked, but I can answer all the ones you are afraid to ask. Yes, you need to move out, because you are living with another woman's husband. Yes, you need to move out because you are telling yourself and your girls that this is okay behavior. If one of your girls came home and told you their situation and it was exactly like yours, what would you tell them? I know this is hard to hear, but you can't wait on Jack Wayne to tell you how to live your life. He is no longer responsible for you. You are responsible for you. If you don't like the scenario you're living in, then you change it, you are responsible for you!" With tears streaming down her face, she said, "Yeah, but I am also responsible for those girls, and I am trying to protect them." "Well, honey, living with another woman's husband and hanging around waiting to see if he is going to get a divorce or not, is no way to protect them. Kids learn what they live, and like I said, do you want them to make the same choices you have made up to this point? Do you want them to think their worth comes from waiting around to see if someone chooses them or not?" I paused and she shook her head no. I continued, "Ok, then you are the only one that can tell them any different." I hugged her and got into my car with tears streaming my own face. This was all just a sad, heavy, miserable road. Once again, Jack stood in the same place he had stood a year and a half ago, with every road ahead of him paved with pain, no matter what path he chose.

In the midst of all of this pain and crazy, little Avery was back in the hospital. He had something going on with a gland on the side of his face. Earlier in the year when they had run all the tests, they discovered that he had a genetic immune disorder. Alivia's dad had suffered with this, as well as her nephews. Since he had this immune disorder, this gland issue caused a bit more of a scare than usual. Jack had promised Alivia he would go to the hospital evaluation with her so that she didn't have to be alone. There was hell to pay for that. With every day Jack remained married, and every doctor's appointment Jack and Alivia went to, a piece of Rachel died. She worried every day that Jack was changing his mind, I think she worried she was changing her mind. Jack wasn't the only one disappointed that coming home hadn't turned out to be all they had expected. Her fear and insecurity were working overtime. What she didn't realize is that while she was anticipating all that she thought might happen, she was missing the opportunity to love the man that had loved her enough to hurt someone who had never wronged him and had done nothing but love him more than he deserved. Rachel wasn't the beautiful sun kissed girl in the gym anymore who was longing to catch the eye of the farm boy in the doorway. She was now among the walking wounded, continually anticipating the death of the love she had finally gotten back. Their love had been on life support and she was standing with her hand on the plug.

Jack, now, not feeling the love he once felt from Rachel, was still dragging his feet to finalize the divorce. He was wading waist deep through his guilt. He wasn't ready to give up his friendship with Alivia, and maybe he was wrestling even giving up his relationship with her, I honestly didn't know. I did know the struggle was real and it was all over the man in his face and in his posture, which was typical of him. When I thought about it, it's really the only way I had known him. I wondered if there would be a day we could exist and be happy, and not be wading through a crisis and living in constant pain and misery. It was like we were right where we were the year before, just on the other side of the fence. The man just hated to hurt people. What he wasn't realizing was that choosing to withhold hurting Alivia, was not only killing Rachel, but it was hurting Alivia, too.

Alivia had been spending a lot of time down at the house. Jason had gotten to spend a lot of time with her lately. Jason knew I had found a good friend in her, and he was happy for me. Every dinner that we ate, game we played, and tractor Jason put together for Avery, his love for them grew more and more. This growing love was evident just a few weeks before Christmas. Avery would be going in to have his ear surgery. Alivia was very nervous, and had decided she would drive up to the city overnight so she didn't have to get Avery up so early the morning of surgery. She had asked me to go, normally before I committed to such things, I would run them by Jason of course, and since it involved Alivia, I would run it by Jack. I knew Jason didn't like for me to be gone overnight, and it would be a struggle for him to get the girls to school and stuff the next morning, so I didn't even run it by him. I apologized to Alivia and told her I just couldn't do it. I would be happy to be there with them during the surgery day, but I wouldn't be able to stay the night. She acted as if no worries, but I could tell she was worried in the tone of her voice.

I had to swing back by her house to pick up some pallets before she headed to the city. Jason helped me load them up. Jason rounded the corner to get his next pallet, and as he turned the corner of the barn Alivia was hugging me and crying. Alivia was nervous about Avery going under anesthesia. Fear paralyzed her, as she closed her eyes and could see her dad lying there lifeless after complications from his surgery. When Jason and I got back in the truck, he asked, "She's going up to the city tonight?" "Yeah," I answered. He quickly questioned me, "Why don't you just go with her?" "Well, she asked me to go, but I knew it would put you in a bind, so I told her I would just go up in the morning," I answered. He never took his eyes off the road and he said, "Well I think you need to go with her, the girls and I will be alright." I immediately called Alivia, "Hey, I will meet you up there. I'm going to run home and get the girls settled and pick up my car." With much relief in her voice she said, "Ok, I'm heading up there now, I will meet you at the hotel." I ran home and grabbed my bags. I never even thought about calling Jack, I knew he would be ok with me going. I started my drive up to the city and my phone rang, it was Danny. We visited almost the entire drive, just catching up and hearing about his progress, it was a nice drive. I text Jack when I got to the city and told him I would see him in the morning, but that I was staying with Alivia at the hotel to help her with Avery in the morning. He was glad she wasn't there alone, and I was glad to be able to help my brother out.

The morning came early, Alivia and I made our trip to Starbucks before we headed to the hospital. We pulled into Children's Hospital and waited patiently. Within just a few minutes, Avery's little voice started chanting, "Dada, Dada's feed truck," which sounded more like "Dada's teed tuck." He was right, there he was. Jack Wayne had pulled into that citified parking lot in that flat-bed feed truck. He quickly got out of the truck and made his way toward the car. He sat in the back seat with Avery and they played and talked. Alivia just smiled, and she and I continued to chat. KK and Pop pulled up and we headed toward the automatic sliding doors of the hospital. The walk was somewhat awkward, KK was trying to figure out how I was already here and why I was in the car with Alivia. I had kept the details of mine and Alivia's friendship somewhat private. KK was really rooting for Rachel and Jack to make this work, for the girls, she would say. She had no idea the misery everyone was living in. She had mentioned to me in the past that she felt like the friendship that Alivia and I shared was causing problems for Rachel and Jack. Since that day, I kept my friendship quiet. I never lied about my friendship with Alivia, it's just not something I willingly shared with KK, it just caused her worry and anxiety that she didn't need to have.

We all sat in the waiting room, anxiously awaiting Avery's turn. The nurse came out, and held her folder up, "Avery Wayne." Jack and Alivia got up and headed through the double doors. KK, Pop, and I sat and waited in the small family waiting area. We hadn't been sitting there too long and Pop said he was going to go find the bathroom. As soon as Pop was out of sight, KK questioned, "So what time did you get here?" "I actually stayed with Alivia and Avery last night at the hotel so I could help her with him this morning," I answered. "Hmm," she said, then what came out of her mouth, actually surprised me, "well it's hard for me to believe that you're the best friend that she has?" She asked it, as somewhat of a question. "I'm probably not the best friend that she has, but since they knew that Jason and I would be coming to the surgery, I was just a logical choice," I answered unapologetically. Pop was making his way around the corner about this time, so KK quickly said, "Oh, well that makes sense, I guess." Pop made his way back to his seat, and we never mentioned that conversation again.

The next few weeks were full of doctor's appointments and lots of times Jack and Alivia would be together. On the days when Jack wasn't at the doctor with Alivia and Avery, Jason would try to help Jack get caught up on feeding all the cattle. Jason had continued to develop his relationship with Avery and Alivia, which led him to a very defining moment in the truck with Jack. "You have to choose man," Jason said, never taking his eyes off the window, as to avoid making contact with Jack. They both just kept looking out the dirty windshield of that feed truck. Jack finally looked away from the road long enough to glance at Jason and ask, "What do you mean?" "Seriously? Man you know what I mean. Either you want to be with Rachel or you want to be with Alivia, but you can't keep them both. If you choose Rachel, that's fine, but you need to let Alivia go. She deserves to find someone who will love her and help her raise that boy," Jason answered. In his short, irritated tone that he got when he didn't like something you have said, Jack asked, "What do you mean raise the boy? I'm his dad, and I'm here." "I understand that, but the reality is you see that boy eight days a month, which means that the man who marries Alivia will be spending twenty-two days a month with him, so yes he will be helping raise him," Jason answered. As Jason was relaying the story to me, I inquisitively asked, "Well, then what did he say?" "Nothing, he was done! You know how he is!" Jason said, very matter-of-fact, and that was the end of that. It was the truth. Sometimes the truth is hard to hear, but it doesn't make it less true. Delaying his decision was also dragging Alivia along, with a hope that he would walk through that door one of those eight days a month and choose to stay. If that wasn't an option, then he needed to sign those papers and let her go.

Day by day, another piece of Rachel was gone. Another day of doubt, and a piece of her died, another silent night, lying in bed next to each, but so alone. As the pieces of her began to get buried, he stopped seeing the girl he fell in love with. He didn't understand what one piece of paper could do for their relationship. Rachel struggled with more than just the fact that Jack was still married, she had many other demons she was wrestling as well. I had a tendency to not be able to see some of Rachel's pain, as I wanted to protect my brother. I failed many times to see his faults and his weaknesses. When you have your battle gear on and your gun drawn waiting to protect someone, it's hard to hear. It's hard to hear the heart of someone else breaking, and it's extremely hard to admit that the one you have been protecting so long, may be the one causing some of that pain. As these painful days passed, I felt more pain than I had ever felt walking through any of my own storms in life. I wanted to love and protect my brother, I wanted him to be whole again. I wanted him to feel love and to quit wallowing in the pit of confliction and chaos.

17

No Happily
Ever After

At this point I honestly had no idea what Jack would do, or truly if he would ever have peace on earth, this side of heaven. It was Sunday morning, I sat on the porch and I told the Lord I had done all I could do. I had gone into the war zone with my guns drawn, I had gotten up every morning at 6 AM praying God's Will in the lives of all involved. I had distanced myself from Rachel, I could see the hurt she was causing Jack, and surprisingly I had somewhat distanced myself from Jack. I was working hard to unbiasedly take them to God because I had no idea, once again what the right answer was. Although I was hurt and wounded from Rachel, I wasn't treating the wound and dealing with it. Instead of talking to her about the problem, I let that wound fester and get infected. I would not apologize for loving Jack, I was not sorry for that. I was also not sorry for the friendship that I had with Alivia. She was a good friend to me, a sweet, kind soul, someone I shared a lot in common with. As I struggled to know what the right counsel was, or what Jack should do, I was reminded of a prayer I had prayed the summer before. Just about a week after Alivia's dad had passed away, Jack was at the same church service as Jason and I, sending the girls off to camp. When I got to the service I found a passage in my Bible about carrying other's pain and misery. I wrote Jack's name next to that passage in my Bible and I prayed that if God would allow me to carry his pain and misery for just one day, so he could rest, I would do it. Today I was regretting that prayer. If this is how Jack Wayne felt, constantly torn between two people, two friends, two heartbeats and two souls, well then I wanted to holler up to God and tell him I wanted to take back my prayer. It was getting uncomfortable and a little painful, I wanted a ticket out. I didn't know how this man had made it this long on this road.

Christmas was just a few weeks away, and the tension between Jack and Rachel continued to grow. KK had planned a big Christmas event for all of us. Jack had been spilling his guts to Jason every day as they drove those back roads and counted calves. Jack had been wrestling with God, the prayers were working. He told Jason that after Christmas, Rachel was going to move out. He was still so conflicted. One day he would tell us that she was moving out, because it was the right thing to do, but they were still going to try and work it out. The next day he came and told us that Rachel told him that she would agree to work on it, but if something fell in her lap, she was more than likely going to go for it. That statement infuriated me, and made me sad for Alivia. Why is it that Rachel wasn't willing to fight for him at all, but he was willing to fight for her? Alivia had given up the last year and a half of her life to wait and fight for Jack, and he was still not willing to fight for her. It might have been the first time ever in the history of our entire friendship that I might have been, for just a few seconds, mad at him. I also knew how he operated, everything had to be his idea, and on his terms, you couldn't just roll up in his driveway and say, "Hey you're an idiot! This is what you need to do!" So I stepped back, loved him, and pleaded with God for him to not let this one go! Jack Wayne was a good man, he deserved the love he had, I don't know what kept him from believing it. That man was wrestling the Lord like a mad man in a caged fight.

With the most sarcasm you can imagine, let me just say, Christmas events were loads of fun. Rachel kept her distance from all of us. We played games, she stood across the room with her arms folded across her chest, and a look that could send anyone straight to hell if looks had any kind of power.   The rest of us had lots of fun, we played Minute to Win It, and KK and Pop's house was full of laughter.   The normal magic was felt by those who were in the dark about what was going on.   For those of us in the light, it made it a bit more of a challenge to have fun, but we got the job done.

KK was still completely in the dark as far as I knew.   Usually, I tried to prepare her for these kinds of blows, but I knew where she stood, and I didn't have the freedom to tell her the things I knew yet. This was Jack's story to tell, I would wait for him to tell it.   As painful as I expected the news of Rachel moving out to be, there was a part of my spirit that was happy.   I didn't know what Jack would choose.   I was just happy he was moving Rachel out, choosing to spend some time getting his head clear, and visiting the idea of dating his wife again.   One thing I had finally put together about this whole puzzling situation the last several months was this... Rachel loved the man Jack was when he was loved by Alivia.   Rachel didn't possess the ability or the capacity to love Jack the way Alivia did.   Alivia's love was unconditional.   Although she knew a part of Jack's heart would forever belong to Rachel because they shared children and history, she was willing to love the part of him she had.   Her love encouraged him, it built him up, it was the steady, strong love that had gotten him back on his feet after Rachel destroyed his world the first time.

Rachel walked away from Jack with no regret, she never looked back. Before she even had all of her stuff moved out, she was loving someone else. She was searching for her identity, her worth, and her purpose in the love of a man. I felt sorry for her, and I say this with sadness, not judgment.

I kept trying to figure out what had changed with Rachel. How was it that a year and a half ago, she was heartbroken and sad, and wanted so badly to have her family back, and now she was right back where she was when she destroyed his life the first time? I watched Jack change as he let Alivia back in through the illness of Avery. I saw his heart soften, I saw his pride crumble, I saw his confidence boost, and I begin to see glimpses of the man I knew was in there all along. The man I could see when he would show us his heart. The man I believed to be an amazingly good man, but he could never see that. He couldn't see it because when he was with Rachel, he bore Rachel's struggles and her pain. When he was loved by Alivia he took on her strength and her goodness. It finally made sense. The man that Jack became when he was loved by Alivia is the man Rachel wanted, but when he was no longer loved by Alivia, he became a man no one wanted. The biggest problem for Rachel is that she couldn't have the man she wanted because she was completely incapable of helping him be that man.

The next week flew by and it was the day before New Year's Eve. Jack had told Jason that morning at the barn that they would be telling the girls, KK and Pop on New Year's Eve that Rachel would be moving out. Jason wanted me to be out of town, and wanted us to be able to just enjoy some time away. Jason and Jack agreed not to tell me until we were already gone.

We made our way to a beautiful secluded cabin. We began carrying our bags inside and Jason made sure we had no phone service, then he said, let's take a walk and see how pretty this lake is. We stepped outside and took just a few steps and he said, "Jack and Rachel are telling the girls tonight that Rachel's moving out." My heart sank, but yet I was happy for Jack. I felt like this was his chance to clear his head and see that Alivia had truly loved him in a way that he could never probably really comprehend. That's what I wanted to allow myself to feel, but at the same time, I felt like I was back having that same lecture I had previously had with Jason so many times, "Haley, you can't pick sides, you never know what he is going to do!!" Surely he understood that when Rachel said, "Yeah, we can work on it, but if something falls in my lap I'm going for it," it was her reminding him that she was in it for her. She was in this as long as it worked for her and fulfilled her needs, but she wasn't in it for the long haul. Unfortunately, she was still that girl she was the first time. There were still moments though, that I felt like he was going to continue to fight for her.

Saturday night Jason and I made it back home and we all went to Danny's to play darts and ring in the New Year together. I still acted like I was clueless, which wasn't a hard act for me. I was standing in Danny's kitchen making my plate. Jack was standing behind me, smacking in my ear, and aggravating me as usual. At one point, he might have been holding a meatball very close to my ear. I was afraid to turn my head and look, so I worked really hard to ignore him. I elbowed him and a little bit of his tea spilled on his shirt. He raised his voice and acted like he was mad, he was trying to keep from laughing, and he said, "Sis, don't be messing up my clothes, I have to do my own laundry now!" I just rolled my eyes and acted like I had no idea what he was talking about, "What are you talking about?" I asked. "What?" he leaned down, as to lower his voice so the whole party didn't hear, he got closer to my ear, where earlier the meatball dangled and asked, almost in a panic, "Jason didn't tell you? He was supposed to tell you once you guys got out of town." I raised my eyebrow and just gave him the look we exchanged often when we both know something that other people in the room might not know. After we exchanged "the look" he knew I was in the loop. He quickly got quiet and headed out to the garage. When he got to the door that went from the kitchen to the garage, he nodded me out there with him. I stepped into the garage and when I turned to shut the door, I nodded Jason out with us. He nodded me on and said he would be there in a minute, he was chatting with someone. I shut the door between the garage and the kitchen, jumped up on the freezer, and began swinging my legs. Jack was standing in the middle of the garage closing one eye and squinting with his open eye, looking down the backside of his dart to the dartboard. I continued swinging my legs, like a little girl, and with an upbeat, unsuspecting voice, I quizzed my big brother, "So what's going on?" He never took his eye off his dart, "Oh you know, the normal," he answered as he threw the dart. It hit the wall, he murmured a cuss word under his breath, and then looked at me with his ornery grin and said, "Well, that's about right." We both laughed. He then told me about Rachel's statement, which opened the door for me to tell him my thoughts. I did my typical sister speech about how he was better than that and he deserved better. I squished my forehead together, making a frown line in between my eyes, and asked, "You hear yourself right now, right? You hear yourself telling me that Rachel told you that she would work it out with you, unless something came and dropped in her lap, then she was going for it? Do you hear it like I'm hearing it?" He picked up another dart, gave me a quick glance, like he had no idea what I was trying to get at, and said, "What do you mean?" He continued throwing his darts, man he was horrible, collecting them and going back to throw them again, the cycle continued over and over as we talked. "What I mean is, I understand you have made your fair share of mistakes, and although I like to think you're the Batman of every story, I know from time to time you can be the Joker. I don't like to admit that about you, as everyone says," I giggled, and he smiled his big goofy smile, and raised his eyebrows, like he knew he was Batman. I continued, "But seriously, you love well Jack. You're a good man, you have a good heart, you have made some bad choices, and yes, you will have to pay some consequences, but God bless, you deserve someone who is going to love you, fight for you, and work at it. Not someone who is going to," I paused again, trying to decide how to say this, I decided air quotes were definitely necessary here, so I raised my hands in the most dramatic way and held up air quotes as I continued, "wait for the next best thing to come around!" He continued back and forth to the dartboard. As he launched his next dart, which was pretty close to the bulls eye, he said, "Hell, I don't know what I'm doing." I couldn't believe it, I honestly thought he would be relieved. They had told the girls, and now he could get his head about him and have his house to himself, and try and figure this mess out. Who did he want to be with? What did he want? I felt like in a sense he already knew the answer, well that's how I felt before we started this conversation. I just didn't understand how one person could hurt you so much, and basically tell you they were just waiting for someone else to come along, and you be willing to keep your heart and your mind in that tortured state. I didn't understand, and he didn't deserve it, but he would have to make that decision for himself. There were some things I just couldn't do for him, but, boy it was painful to watch.

Sunday we all awkwardly went to church. The girls went to lunch at the same place we did. They were done and left before we even started eating. We were finishing up our lunch and my phone began ringing. It was Baylee, "Aunt Haley, I left my retainer on the table in a napkin, can you grab it for me?" "Sure!" I answered as I was running to the table where they had sat. The bus boy was already putting the napkin that was holding the retainer inside his bucket of trash. I caught him just in time. I laughed, anticipating telling Baylee what had happened. We finished up our lunch and Jason said he would swing me by to drop the retainer off to Baylee.

Jason stayed in the car when we parked in Jack's driveway and told me to run it in. I opened the door and then realized that today was the day. Today was the day Rachel was moving out. Some of her stuff was already gone, the house already felt a bit emptier. Jack stood at the sink, with his hand in a pot of water, he kept stirring it around and around but his eyes never left the window. I told him I was there to bring Baylee her retainer, he nodded me back and said, "She's back there." His eyes still never left the window. I told Baylee the whole story, we laughed, she took her retainer and went straight back to her room. I walked around the big island in the kitchen and I went to give him a quick hug. As I reached around to side hug his shoulder, I asked, "You okay?" His eyes still never left the window, but he began sobbing uncontrollably. "Hey, hey," I said, wanting him to look my way. He never did, so I continued, as if he were looking right at me. "Hey, you're going to be ok, do you hear me? We are going to be ok. Jack, look at me," I pleaded. He finally peeled his eyes away from the window and looked into my eyes, still no words, just the sounds of painful sobs. His tall, lean body just shook with every sob. "We are going to be fine, do you hear me? Jason and I are right here. Do you see me standing here?" I asked. He never spoke he just nodded his head. "We are going to be right here, as long as you keep stepping forward. God is a God of forward motion, and as long as you are moving forward we are going to be right here with you. Listen to me, you have three kids in this mess, they all need you to keep moving forward, one step at a time, one day at a time, you got it?" He nodded again. "Listen to me, Brother, you are going to be fine. You are going to be more than fine." After I made this statement, I then asked him another question, and this time I wanted an answer, "Do you believe me?" He just glared at me with a blank lost look on his face, so I asked him again, "Do you believe me? Jack, nod your head if you believe me." As his body continued to shake and the short sounds of audible sobs came from his mouth, he looked at me and nodded his head yes. I hugged him as tight as I could and told him I loved him. I walked out of the house, leaving a part of my heart with him there at the sink.

I can't remember if I actually ran, but I wanted to. I got to the car as quickly as I could and I told Jason he had to go in. I started crying and then pleading with Jason, "You have to go in and help him. He's so sad. It's so sad, I just don't even know how to help him." Jason said, "We will run home and pick up his trailer that I need to bring back, so it doesn't look like I'm just going right in there after you to check on him." We ran home, picked up the trailer, and then headed back. There was a slight problem when we got back close to Jack's house, Rachel was there with KK and Pop loading up the truck with more of Rachel's things and pieces of Jack's life. Jason said, "Nope, we are staying out of that one. We will come back later." KK was still upset. She thought all of this was Jack's fault for not getting divorced. Jack helped get everything loaded and waited for Rachel to leave the driveway to tell Mom and Dad the truth. The truth was Jack hadn't gotten the divorce, the other part of the truth was that Rachel had been seeing someone. KK was devastated, but at the same time she was in denial. She tried for several weeks to have talks with them and try and make this thing happen, but the thing was, this had been over shortly after it had started. I think they hung on as long as they had for the sake of the girls. KK is a fixer, though, and she was convinced she was going to fix them. She couldn't, no one could. This struggle was something they would have to do on their own.

For a couple of weeks, Jack tried to work on his relationship with Rachel. Then one night I got a text, "I'm done!" "Ok?" I replied. I had been done the night we stood in Danny's garage, and maybe I had been done before then. The moment I realized that Jack's heart was bleeding, but he continued to fight and try for this girl and she did not reciprocate his efforts at all, I was done. I stayed in the game for Jack, his relationship was worth it for me. "Went by her shop today, there was another guy there. She's not trying to work this out. I'm done!! Told her I don't want to work on it now. I'm done!" I'm still not sure why he was surprised, or what he expected when she said, "If something falls in my lap," what exactly he didn't understand about all that, I didn't know. Maybe it was just the protection of denial, that thing we were all familiar with; when we know something in our head but we keep our heart in that place of denial to try and prolong the protection and keep ourselves from feeling the inevitable pain awaiting us. I was happy that he understood now, rather sooner than later, and now he could close that chapter of his life and quit trying to drive his car forward while staring in his rearview. I'm a gal all for a rearview mirror, I think it's necessary sometimes in life to take a quick glance at where we've been, while still moving forward in our motion, but I'm not gonna lie, I would have loved to rip his rearview mirror right out of his vehicle.

I'm sure it was easier for me to look ahead, my heart wasn't as involved as his was, and I knew what lay ahead. I had walked in Alivia's closet one day to borrow a shirt, and I had seen the pieces of paper with prayers for that man from top to bottom of that closet. I had witnessed her strong, steady love for him, and I had seen her heart and not one ounce of anger or bitterness was found there when it came to him. I loved the man, he was my number three, there was God, Jason, and Jack, but I'm just going to say what we are all thinking: If he had done to me what he had done to Alivia, I probably would have already killed the man and buried him myself. I sure wouldn't have a closet full of prayers and a longing to return to his arms. Alivia's love was steady for Jack, her forgiveness was already granted, and I knew that was an option in the road ahead for him. I was ready for him to put the pedal to the metal and get us out of this reckless vehicle that had been traveling in reverse at a high rate of speed for the past year and a half.

18

On the Road Again

The next few weeks were rough. Jack Wayne didn't do alone well. He struggled, but the Lord continued to wrestle him, and match by match, the Lord was winning. It had been almost a month since Rachel had moved out now. It was hard to trudge through this during basketball season. In those bleachers there were so many memories, and every game Rachel was there. Our seating assignments were much different this season, and there were no long, loving gazes being exchanged. This week we had a tournament which meant we would get to share this awkward moment four days this week, instead of the usual two. Jack walked into the gym Thursday night holding Avery. Avery was like a soothing, healing balm to all of our open wounds, and he was the best distraction for all of the tension that filled the gym. Every time I saw that little man he lit up the room, and I couldn't help but wear a smile when he was around. Jason and I sat behind Jack and Avery: KK, Pop, and Danny sat next to him. As Avery would get restless, we would all take turns passing him around, trying to help Jack out. The game was almost over, the gym was humid and stuffy, and Avery's blonde hair line began to show signs of sweat. He never cried, but he was getting tired and more restless than he had been the first half. Jack began collecting his things, Jason and I helped pack up the bags, and Peyton hollered, "Dad, I want to ride with you to take Avery home." "Ok," he said, "let's go!" I reached down to hand him Avery's other bag, as my hand went to pass the bag off to him, he looked me in the eyes with those vulnerable, "go ahead and peek into my soul" eyes, and said, "Thank you for helping me with him." I smiled and said, "Of course." His sensitivity to thanking me was not his normal self. Although it did make me happy for him to be so thankful, it also made me sad, as it was a painful reminder of how alone he was.

Jason and I headed home. I played that moment over and over in my head, and then a text interrupted my play-by-play moment with yet another play-by-play moment, "Man, this food is good. I needed this. Can't get Peyton to leave." By this point, I knew my brother well. This was him asking me if it was ok for him to be there, to be enjoying a meal with Alivia, Avery, and Peyton. It was his way of asking me what I thought. "Well, Brother, I'm happy for you, and I don't blame Peyton, I don't ever want to leave when I'm there either. It's always great food and amazing company." That's all he needed to know! It was okay to be enjoying that moment, and he did. That meal was the beginning of many meals they would start to share, as Alivia did what she had always done. She would pack up her husband, begin to patch him up, and slowly, but surely, her strong and steady love would get him back on his feet again. Just like that, Alivia began collecting the pieces of Jack's heart and life, and steadily she started putting him back together again, piece by piece.

With every sunrise, Jack Wayne became a man I had never had the privilege to see. He was funnier than I had remembered, he smiled more, and he was more kind and aware of what was going on. He would send me messages for no reason, telling me he was thankful for me and our relationship. He would check on me when I was having to go to funerals where my dad would be attending. He was considerate and kind, and not buried and crushed under the weight of the misery and pain he had been carrying around so long. Although this detour had been so painful, and I am sure that to Alivia it felt like forever on the timeline of her life, I felt like it was essential. Jack was a "my way or the highway" kind of guy. He had to see and learn things on his own, he wasn't the "take you for your word" kind. He longed to fix his life and his marriage with Rachel, and as long as his mind played in the playground of what might have

233

been, I am not sure he could have ever loved Alivia the way she deserved. His detour allowed him to get the answers he needed, it confirmed for him that the love there was lost, and it was dead. Although there were many good things that had come from that love and that marriage, it was now in the rearview of his life. He could no longer travel in reverse, he realized it was a death trap for him to continue to do so. This detour cost him some time and some pain, but it also allowed him to lose some baggage along the way that had kept him beat down and defeated. Dumping the baggage allowed him the freedom to love with his whole heart and to begin to truly heal.

He would forever carry the scar that the love he lost with Rachel had left, but he was no longer a bleeding heart. He was healing. With every sunrise, I saw strength, and just like the trees outside began to bud and get new life, so was it for the heart of Jack Wayne.

This detour had truly been tragic to this farm boy. It had torn apart his heart and soul, and shredded them in several thousand different pieces. The only way he had made it through this mess was to hold tight to the hand of Jesus and trust Him to wade him through his pain, doctor his wounds, and bring restoration to his life. Jesus was the original blood brother of our group. Although Danny and Jack didn't realize it, what connected us the most was our wounds. Not just the wounds that we had inflicted on ourselves that night around the campfire when we decided to become blood brothers and sister, but the wounds this world had lashed out on us as we had traveled its path. Our wounds are what connects us, our willingness to let love in is what heals us, and our decisions to walk this hard, cold road together is what leads us down the road to restoration. One day, when we see Jesus face to face, we will truly be healed, but until then we have to realize the journey is just as important. The journey is where champions are made, hearts are mended, and character is built. No matter how tragic our detours in life have been, currently are, or are going to be in the future, we have to keep fighting to find our way home. Fighting to put God back where He belongs in our lives, fighting to put God in the center of our marriages and our hearts, because He is the only kind of glue that holds everything together. Jack would continue on his journey, different than when he had started, and because of his detour my life, too, would never be the same. His detour had led him on a path that allowed his life road to intersect with mine and that was something I would forever be thankful for. On a detour, you see things and you go places you may have never intended to see or go. Sometimes on a detour, you find exactly what you need, and sometimes you don't, but either way you can't stop traveling. What's done is done, and you have to move forward and face the consequences of your decisions, good or bad. Love is messy, it hurts, and sometimes we feel like it may bring us to our death, but the truth about love is that it "keeps no record of wrong, it ALWAYS protects, always trusts, always hopes, and always perseveres – 1 Corinthians 13:5." We are all the same in our struggles, we are vulnerable and weak, and unstable in our thoughts and in our ways. We are irrational, and sometimes we are just plain mean to the people we love. We all have wounds, some make the decision to hide them, others make the life giving decision to rub them up against yours and commit to walking through this battle in life together. I can't understand love, and I am not going to waste another minute trying. When we try to figure out love with our heads, we lose it all together. Love isn't a head thing, it's a heart thing. I am going to allow God to deal with the stuff in my life that has built walls around my heart so that I can love the people He has given me, and I can love them well. I'm going to allow God to get real with me so he can begin tearing down that detour sign and help me get back on the path He wants me to travel. I don't understand the cross. I don't understand the love I have for my own children. I don't understand the unconditional love my husband has for me. I sure don't understand the bond that the Lord nurtured and grew between me and the farm boy, but I accepted the gift with my heart and didn't try to understand it all with my head. I am so glad that I made that choice. God uses relationships in our lives to help us heal, grow, experience love, and to see a glimpse of Him every day. Without relationships, we are just wreckage. Don't lose heart, don't stop traveling your road. If you are on a detour in life, keep pressing on, travel through, find some road trip buddies who will help you find your way, or at least encourage you and love you as you work on finding it. Love is not an option, it's a necessity, right up there with oxygen. We only get one shot at this life, may we travel our road well and may we travel with many. May we let go of our false hopes of a shallow fairy tale and may we fight to leave a legacy of love.

Acknowledgements

First I want to thank God for all He has done for me. For all the healing and restoring He has done in my own life and for all the people he has used to accomplish that!

To my husband, Josh Abbott, who is always supportive of whatever crazy dream I have and who has loved me unconditionally for over half of my life. He has been my constant in the midst of my chaos and he has been steady to love me through my own insecurities. He truly loves in a way that is unexplainable! He also intentionally works to make me laugh everyday and that alone is worth a lot! Babe, you are the real MVP!!

To my two girls, Jayden and Taylor for their excitement and encouragement to tackle this dream! I love you both. You make me better.

To my Wing T family, thanks for picking up all the slack at work while I finished this project, and for all your faith in me and pushing me to tell the story. A special thanks to Jennifer Heavin, who helped do edits, and Britton Hill who designed my cover and helped me with all this techy stuff I don't understand!! I honestly wouldn't be walking in any of my dreams without you girls!

To Amanda Scott at Crosslight Photography for just being an amazing person and for capturing exactly what I wanted on the front cover!!

To ALL my friends who have been so encouraging to me since the moment I began this journey!!

Last, but not least, to my brother, thank you for allowing me to tell your story. Thank you for loving the mess I am, and for teaching me its ok to let walls down and its safe to let love in. Although this detour was extremely painful, I will forever be grateful that it led me to you!